STO

THE SORCERER

THE SORCERER

by Anne Eliot Crompton

illustrated by Leslie Morrill

An Atlantic Monthly Press Book
Little, Brown and Company
BOSTON   TORONTO

LIBRARY OF CONGRESS CATALOG CARD NO. 70–150048

FIRST EDITION

T 08/71

ATLANTIC–LITTLE, BROWN BOOKS
ARE PUBLISHED BY
LITTLE, BROWN AND COMPANY
IN ASSOCIATION WITH
THE ATLANTIC MONTHLY PRESS

Published simultaneously in Canada
by Little, Brown & Company (Canada) Limited

PRINTED IN THE UNITED STATES OF AMERICA

THE SORCERER

ONE

THE SPIRIT

1

A WHISPER in gentle air, a momentary flicker among golden grasses — was it movement? Or was it only the startle of her timid heart?

Grass still clamped in strong determined jaws, the pony mare swung up her head. Standing straight and still, she looked into the quiet autumn noon. She looked up the near slope, where brown grasses waved among patches of early snow. She looked through the sunlight that warmly dappled the gray rocks and glinted in the grass. A light wind stirred.

Uneasily the mare chomped, looking about. Then

she swallowed her mouthful and wrinkled her soft nose to the breeze which came meandering down the slope. It brought a strong smell of pony: of sweat, hot horsehair, and stallion.

Very faintly the mare detected another scent on the soft wave of air — a perplexing, unplaceable scent. She snorted, clearing her nose, and stretched out her head on its short neck and tried again.

It was, after all, a pony smell. And it was stale. Now the mare understood that a dead pony lay somewhere over the hilltop, a stiff dark shape rotting in brown grass. As the scent became clear and reassuring the breeze died.

But still the mare was restless. She was a heavy, compact creature with a strong bite and a savage kick; she could take care of herself. But her soul was still that of her ancestors — tiny, graceful animals, whose only defense was instant flight. From these timid little beings she inherited extreme wariness and caution. So now she pricked up her ears, one forward, one back, to catch the slight sounds of noon: flies buzzing, ponies chewing, the *hrrrm* of a distant herd-fellow.

And once more the mare looked intently about for the stealthy shadow she thought she had seen. She looked directly toward Lefthand.

He sensed her gaze aimed at the hillock behind

which he crouched. He trembled. If he did not clamp his teeth shut they would chatter. The hand that gripped the spear shook hard, and he had to press it against the ground to stop its jiggling.

But Lefthand knew that excitement, like fear, could travel through air and betray him. The mare's thought, vaguely spreading toward him, must not meet his own thought driving at her like a spear. He must relax. He looked down at the dead grass around his knees, at the autumn light rippling on the rock under his hand. He drew a long silent breath and tried to think about something less exciting.

The first image that came to mind was that of his father's hand, pointing. "Lefthand," he seemed to hear his father say, "you and Onedeer creep down the north side. Remember, go *slowly*. We will be coming up on the south side. Start throwing when you hear the wolf howl." Provider had pointed out the strategy with a strong jabbing finger. His hand did not tremble, his voice was steady. It might have been the game, "you be the pony," that Lefthand had played through his childhood, but it was not.

Lefthand squirmed forward on his stomach to the brow of the hill overlooking this hollow. Parting the grass with careful fingers he peered through and down and immediately felt sick!

The ponies were real. Fat and solid in the early morning sunshine, their shadows dark beside them, they were scattered far across the hollow like pebbles tossed by a carefree hand. Beside Lefthand on the hilltop, Onedeer hissed astonishment. He turned his head toward Lefthand and their eyes met, signaling profound excitement. Never before had they seriously stalked real ponies!

The herd was completely relaxed and unsuspecting. All the heads were down, nuzzling in the grass. No hint had reached the ponies of the presence of four hungry people. They did not feel yet the fierce gaze of greed upon them.

When the boys began the long crawl down into the hollow, the sun was low, the morning fresh and cool. Lefthand crept craftily from rock to bush to hillock. Stooping or crawling he hurried across open spaces and dived into coverts. Once hidden, he raised himself cautiously and checked on the herd. Each time he looked, the hollow was nearer, the ponies bigger. If the ponies suspected a moment too soon, all would be lost; the speed of those stubby, galloping legs could not be matched by human strides.

Once a flicker of light caught Lefthand's eye, slanting sunshine glinting momentarily on Onedeer's head. Instantly Onedeer vanished behind a boulder. Another time Lefthand glimpsed a gray mound squirming hastily into a thicket. That was Onedeer's rear end.

Apart and yet together the boys worked their slow, careful way down the hill, stopping short whenever a pony raised its head. Now it was high noon, hot and shrill with fly-song, and Lefthand was within spearing range of the nearest quarry.

By now the men must have reached the top of the opposite hill. In his mind Lefthand saw them. They were rising slowly, cautiously, from a prone crawl to their knees and from their knees to their feet. If they were seen now it might not be disastrous, for they were disguised. Lefthand's father, Provider, wore a black pony skin with the coarse mane flopping down his back. Bisonhorn's pony skin had once been red and white, but it was now so old and worn that the hair had rubbed off. It was a limp, shapeless thing. But it still smelled of stale pony. Lefthand imagined the men slowly standing, raising their spears.

No, that was the wrong thought! He was shaking again, probably reeking of excitement. He must think of something calm.

Deliberately he daydreamed a fire, surrounded by

[7]

night. Low it burned. It sank into embers and in the embers appeared a rounded, blackened shape, crinkled and crisp — a haunch of pony! So vivid was the image that Lefthand wiggled his nose, waiting for the rich smell to flood him with delight . . .

A chomping, pulling sound woke him from his dream.

The mare had decided. All was well. Her timidity had deceived her. Now she had her nose deep in the grass.

Very, very slowly Lefthand raised himself on his knees and spied around the hillock.

Broadside to him, ten steps away, the little brown mare grazed happily. Winter-heavy, her coat hung almost to her knobby knees. Her short, stiff mane bushed over her eyes. Her back and the upper half of her beautiful round barrel gleamed red in the sun. Where her side curved widely down to her belly she was shaded dark, dark brown.

Lefthand could not stop trembling. He shook from hunger, and from the muscular exhaustion of the long crawl. He shook from hope. But most of all he shook from the cold fear of failure.

When Lefthand and Onedeer were little boys they had stalked hares, creeping up behind them as they sat nibbling. But hares had eyes standing out from their heads. The glossy eyes would turn back at the boys while the hare crouched and nibbled. As they came closer the ears would twitch. In that second of indecision, before the hare decided to run, they could jump and catch him. Onedeer had it figured like that, and once he actually did catch a hare. Lefthand would snatch a breath, dart in, and the hare would be off with a flick of his long hind legs and gone. Lefthand would seize grass. He had never caught a hare.

Now he was too old for stalking hares. He was stalking a pony and this time the price of failure would be a cold stomach. The reward of success, on the other hand, would be a charred, crisp pony haunch! There was the haunch, ten strides away. It took a slow step forward, the small hoof daintily lifted and set itself down, as the mare reached for more luscious grass.

Beyond the mare, a shadow twitched. Lefthand blinked. That was no hump of rocky earth piled beside the snow patch! That was a young colt! Brown-stippled white, he lay on brown earth beside white snow and shook his head and cleared his nose and lay still again, fuzzily folded over neat little hoofs. Head up, eyes closed, drenched in sunlight, the colt dozed.

Beyond the colt the slope rose to the near horizon where the men must be waiting. Among the patches of snow and scrub Lefthand saw movement. Here and there stirrings shook light as sound shakes air. A hump of snow wandered onto grass; a tail flicked from a bush. Under the sleepy sun the southern slope was quietly alive with ponies.

Lefthand was gripped from behind. Strong breath panted in his ear. Onedeer had sneaked up without a whisper of sound or a flicker of shadow. Still the mare grazed, moving slowly forward, still turning her lovely broad side to the boys, who knelt together trembling, gripping their spears in sweaty, sticky hands. Would the wolf never call?

Sound shattered air.

Up jerked the mare's head. Her hindquarters tensed. She looked away, upslope from the boys.

Up jerked Lefthand's spear. But Onedeer's grip on his shoulder tightened in a warning clench. It was not the wolf's call they had heard. It was the stallion's call.

Heads rose out of bushes all up and down the hill as the herd came to attention. Black, brown, and gray heads looked up toward the horizon, all the ears pointed, the muzzles muttered. The little colt rocked himself up and came to stand with his mother.

Over the rim of the southern hill a pony came flying. Black against the deep blue air she bounded. She came leaping down and a second pony hurtled onto the skyline. Bigger, blacker, with mane and tail long enough to flap in his wind, the stallion rushed down upon the black mare, shrieking his shivering declaration.

The mare stopped. She threw her weight onto her front feet. Her whole hind end rose into the air as she kicked the stallion in the jaw. Down in the hollow the boys heard the whack.

The stallion rolled back on his heels. He shook his head and came on again. As he reared, the mare doubled quickly under him and bit at his knees. She galloped away at an angle, the stallion up and after her. He circled and came at her from the front, and the two ponies reared and pawed, twisted and bit.

"Now!" thought Lefthand. "Now!"

The herd's attention was centered on the combatants. The brown mare's cheek was turned well away from him, her ears were pricked toward the horizon. Behind her he saw the legs of the colt, and knew that those sharp young eyes were also turned away, looking uphill.

They might move before the wolf called. He might not have a chance like this again. Now was the striking time.

Lefthand drew his spear back, tilting the point

slightly toward the sky, a little higher than the mare's side appeared to be. The spear would describe a neat arc. He rose to his feet.

Onedeer gasped.

The mare caught the motion, a flicker in the corner of her eye. Her pricked ears heard the gasp. She screamed an ear-jarring warning to the herd. She was in flight in the same moment. As Lefthand's spear drove forward in its prescribed arc the mare bounded. At her side the colt jumped, muscles flowing strongly under the baby fuzz.

Instantly the wolf howled. Two figures stood suddenly on the skyline. Shaggy and short, they looked at that distance like two bears.

Spears flew in the moment, two from the hilltop, one from the hollow, as Onedeer and the men cast into the herd.

But even as the spears arced through the air the shocked herd came to life. With warning screams and snorts the ponies flung themselves into flight. The hillside rumbled and shivered under their rush. Lefthand's little brown mare dashed away on shining hoofs as his spear dove harmlessly under her belly. Beyond her Lefthand saw the colt's swift legs gather and stretch.

The thunder passed and stilled. The beautiful, fat

ponies who had cast dark round shadows on the morning earth became fast-flying diminishing specks in the distance.

Now the slope lay empty under the noon sun, bare between the hungry men looking down and the hungry boys looking up.

Four clean bone-tipped spears lay like children's toys, lost in the stubble.

2

The meat rack stood naked in the gray dawn.

Between four gnarled, wind-stunted oaks Provider and Bisonhorn had lashed sapling stakes. The stakes were tied more or less horizontally from tree to tree and crisscross, high enough above the ground to hold long strips of meat for smoking. Around the base of the oaks tools were left lying, ready for joyful use: narrow bone blades, heavier blades, and stone axes. But the rack stood empty, a stark network against the sky. From a distance it might have appeared a natural growth of branches. Like everything else in camp it was slapdash, impermanent, fragile as life itself.

Down from the lowering sky came snowflakes, hesitant and soft. One by one at first, they spiraled down to spatter and melt on the hard earth. But as the cloud cover steadily grayed the white flakes came faster, a shower of light through pale air. They no longer melted as they fell, but flake clung to flake with cold, sticky fingers. They whitened the ground.

The meat rack turned white, its harsh lines softened and fuzzed with snow. The two torn skin tents, leaning feebly together as though for comfort, sagged even farther under the new weight. The fire, dying in its circle of stones, hissed at the snowflakes that fell ever faster into its heart.

Lefthand and Onedeer sat huddled in their skin jackets, staring into the glow. Lefthand was vaguely remembering some dream or vision — something black and hot crackling among embers. If he could keep this picture in his mind, hopefully, his stomach might be deceived and forget that it was empty. He combed his thick dark hair with his fingers and scratched lice. He stared into the fire where vision faded to sad reality. Reality was a sleeping fire, an empty meat rack, a grimly chill morning.

There was some hope. New snow had already

obliterated the boot prints of the departing hunters. Squinting through sleep-heavy eyes from his tent, Lefthand had watched Provider and Bisonhorn go out into the predawn dark. Black silhouettes darting against firelight, they had snatched up their spears, slung bone blades on thongs about their waists, and discussed strategy in whispering grunts. Lefthand had watched Bisonhorn point briefly toward the tents where he and Onedeer still lay, bundled warmly in reindeer robes. He had seen his father's rejecting gesture. "Naaa," he said with his sweeping, outthrust hand, "they can sleep, we don't need *them!*" Bisonhorn agreed with a flap of his hand and the two shadows stalked away, leaving the firelight clear.

Lefthand was reminded of a wolf he had once seen leaping through juniper bushes. He had crouched in a thicket and watched the lean red form leap back again and dodge away at an angle, a streak of red among dark green spikes. Once outside the junipers the wolf paused, in plain view of Lefthand, and looked back. Ears pricked, tail high, he looked where a whining scuffle bent the low bushes. Then he turned and trotted away, expressively satisfied from nose to swinging tail. He went off to hunt by himself, leaving his puzzled cubs sniffling on his trail.

Across the fire Onedeer sniffed, loud and wet, and

then he coughed. Onedeer's eyes were blue, the mild blue of a spring sky, but dull and miserable. Coarse, sunny hair rumpled his head and wisped to his shoulders, hunched under their thin covering and topped with a layer of snowflakes. He sat across the little fire from Lefthand and leaned over it, soaking up warmth. Suddenly he hunched lower, as though trying to hide. Exasperation sharpened his sad eyes.

Out beyond the thickening veil of falling snow a strident, squeaky voice scolded, boasted, laughed. As it came nearer, Onedeer slumped farther and farther under his jacket. If he had had the energy, Lefthand would have laughed.

Out of the snow-mist came the owner of the squeaky voice. Jaybird was little; when they stood together his brown hair brushed Lefthand's ribs. He had Lefthand's brown eyes, but in his round face they were gleeful, snapping eyes. His thin arms clasped a bundle of twigs against his chest. He opened his arms and dropped the twigs in an untidy heap.

Jay did not walk but pranced toward the fire, his ragged cloak flapping about his lean, lifting legs. At the edge of warmth he stopped, drew back his head, stared at Lefthand, and stamped. Then he swished the cloak behind him like a nervous tail.

Lefthand had to smile.

A larger form slowly took shape through the snow. A woman waddled toward Onedeer and dumped an armful of twigs and branches in an orderly pile within reach of the fire. It was Onedeer's mother, Bright. No one ever looked at Bright enough to notice that her once sunny hair was no longer bright, and her face had lost its flashing good cheer. It was still a friendly face, brown like a late autumn valley, with two blue pools shining in its shadows.

Bright squatted by the fire and reached for the sticks. One by one she fed them to the fire until a little flame caught and flickered. Soon the fire began to pop and snap, hissing louder at the falling snow. The boys squirmed closer, leaning to the warmth.

Once the fire was decidedly alive, Bright sank down cross-legged beside it and opened her cloak. Lefthand tensed, waiting for the dreadful sound to come.

The tiny, scrawny infant bundled in the cloak turned its pale face toward the light. With eyes screwed shut and hands clenched in anger or in pain, it opened its mouth amazingly wide and began to scream.

Bright bent over the infant and held it to her warmth, urging it to suck. But the baby was too weak to suck. It could do no more than scream and squirm, writhe its head back and forth, and tremble its little fists. Bright bent close above it, her long tangled hair cloaked it, and on the hair snow began to pile. She was unconscious of snow, of cold, or the watching boys. Her slow patient mind was bent only on feeding and warming her wretched infant.

Jay began to talk. He jumped up and ran around, showing how he had picked up sticks in the thickets. He squeaked and chattered like a squirrel, making a long story of the trip for firewood.

The baby continued to scream, Jay to jabber, the fire to hiss. Lefthand felt the lice crawling in his clothes. Usually he ignored them, but now that his mind was dull and his spirit dim, they were the liveliest things about him. Over the fire his eyes met Onedeer's. There was no need for words. The message was sent and agreement reached in a look.

"Come on, Jay!" Lefthand called. "We're going hunting!"

"Eeeeeeya! Eeeeeeya!" yelled Jay. Waving his arms and jumping like a hare, he ran for his small spear under the meat rack.

Onedeer cast Lefthand an angry look. He would have liked to hop over the junipers and leave the cub sniffing. But he went for his spear and picked up the tools that were almost buried in snow, piling them against an oak trunk.

"Let's go!" Lefthand gestured.

Bent over her baby, Bright never looked up.

3

Falling snow whispered to the stunted firs. Faster it fell, the flakes bigger. Like balls of seed down, they tumbled across the gray skyline, vanished against the white landscape, and reappeared momentarily on cheek and mitten.

Jaybird had never before ventured so far from camp without a grown-up. If she had realized their departure, Bright would not have let them go. While nursing her sick baby, she forgot the world outside her arms. She had forgotten Jay. Lefthand knew she had forgotten them all.

He saw in his mind a picture of her sitting by the fire, crooning hopelessly to the baby. It waved clenched hands and wailed hopelessly at her. Lefthand shuddered. He set his face firmly away from camp and broke into a trot.

He jogged like a young reindeer through the scrub forest. Behind him Jay, breathtakingly happy to be on this adventure. He was so happy, he was silent.

Jay had more energy than the two older boys together. This was because he got more than his share of whatever meat there was. Bright divided hers with him in uneven hunks, the fatter hunk for Jay. Sometimes Provider saved him a specially good tidbit. And even Lefthand found, of late, that he could not hold on to two handfuls of meat while Jay stood and looked at him, the brown eyes suddenly huge in an elongated, pale face. He would chaw on one handful as long as he could, pretending he did not have the other. But somehow it hurt inside, and sooner or later he would see his own hand go out to Jay, with the meat in it.

So now while Lefthand trotted to get away from the sorrowful camp, Jay trotted for the sheer joy of it, bouncing on his strong short legs, feeling the snow soft and springy under his boots. Only Onedeer, bringing up the rear, glanced around with a hunter's eye. Only he watched for tracks, holes, and rotted trees where small animals might hide.

His eye snatched at a tremble of motion. He stopped abruptly.

A large squirrel loped from birch to oak. He held a frozen crab apple just barely gripped in his teeth. He waved along, arching first his body, then his long fuzzy tail. Now he was hidden behind the oak.

Onedeer waited. His eye traveled up the heavy gray trunk to the first crotch, higher than his head. A twitch, a jerk — the squirrel was there.

Onedeer whispered, "*Lefthand!*"

In mid-stride, Lefthand stopped. Jay bumped into him, squealed and at his signal fell silent.

A moment they stood together. Lefthand listened to the whisper of the snow. He looked into his brother's eyes, turned up confidently to his, and knew how it would feel to be grown up.

Then he pushed Jay aside and stole back along the track. He found Onedeer standing quietly, pointing with his chin. Then Lefthand and Jay saw the jerky squirrel motions in the oak crotch. The prey would be hidden in a moment. Nearby there would be a hole down which he could vanish as they watched.

Together Lefthand and Onedeer ran forward and cast their spears.

Perhaps the squirrel, like the boys, was starving. Perhaps his brain was dull. He sat a second longer, gulping his frozen apple though the spears arced close past him, one above, one below.

Looking around for another possible weapon, Lefthand saw Jay poised to throw. He had dropped his spear. In his fist he held a stone. The stone was as big for Jay's hand as the apple was big for the squirrel's mouth. His mitten could barely cup it. His arm could never hurl it.

"No," said Lefthand, and reached for the stone. Jay drew back his arm. The stone slanted darkly into the gray sky.

Clunk. Scrabble. The squirrel fell. Still clutching his apple he turned a somersault in air, tail over head, head over tail, and landed unhurt in the soft snow. But three hungry boys waited for him with spears and stone. Battered from three sides, the squirrel went limp. Stone-bashed behind the ears, it squeaked and leaped once more into the air. It fell limp again and Lefthand stoned it repeatedly on the forehead till the eyes bulged out and blood ran from the open mouth. Then Lefthand straightened, panting.

"It's yours," he said to Jay. "You gut it."

The men always gutted their kills on the spot before bringing them home to the fire, but Jay did not know how.

"Show you," said Lefthand.

He stamped firmly on the tail and stretched out the squirrel. With his bone blade he punched a hole under the tail and slowly worked the point up the belly. Onedeer bent to help him, pulling the valuable skin away from the incision. Now between the opening lips of skin they saw the dark red liver. Steam arose, and a stench. Suddenly the boys felt the hunger that before had been a weak sadness. They felt it as pain in their bellies and nausea in their throats.

Lefthand bit off his mittens. He hooked his fingers into the cavity, grasped the warm bulbs of the still bubbling innards, drew them out and threw them on the snow.

Like hawks diving from the sky, the three boys fell upon the feast.

4

Warmth and appetite flooded Lefthand's body. Again he trotted through the scrub, again Jay came behind, the stiff squirrel impaled upon his spear. His cheeks were red with blood, and with the excitement of success. Watchful Onedeer brought up the rear.

Lefthand stopped suddenly. Before him a huge paw

print was pressed into the snow. He crouched and fitted his own hand into the track. Blunt behind, clawed in front, it could have contained three boys' hands. Even as he squatted, measuring the print, snow fell on his hand and he saw that the track was half filled in.

"We can't follow that!" Onedeer muttered. He stooped over Lefthand. His gaze darted from thicket to tree, awed and cautious.

Jay jabbered softly, "What it is? What is it?"

Lefthand had never seen this track before but he knew as well as Onedeer what it was. He had seen his father draw it in mud, in sand and snow.

"It is the spirit," he told Jay, "the spirit who is our friend." And to Onedeer he said, "We can follow him. He must want us to follow him!"

Lefthand decided, and sprang up. His color was high with triumphant excitement. He pointed his chin along the track that wandered on through the scrub, rapidly vanishing in falling snow.

"He will help us if we follow him — quick!" Not waiting for arguments, he strode off along the spirit track, taking two long steps between each paw mark.

For the first time in his life, Lefthand was elated. He felt like Jay looked, hot and happy. In camp the meat rack stood empty. The last pony herd had rumbled away to the south, the reindeer had not yet come from the north. Now came the spirit, his track in the snow like a rainbow in the sky and he, Lefthand Useless, was the one to find it! Onedeer would never have dared by himself without Lefthand's example. Onedeer's hand was surer than his, Onedeer's eyes were keener. But Lefthand suspected that his own mind was the sharper of the two. Now he could prove it!

The track was clearer now and Lefthand saw that the claw marks alone were as long as his hand. He slowed, peering ahead into the whirling whiteness. He heard the soft, constrained breathing of the others at his back. He stopped. Vague through the dizzy mist he had seen a vast hulk of darkness. Twenty paces ahead it lumbered along. Swaying and waddling, it swung its great head low.

Lefthand opened his hand behind his back and heard Jay gulp down the question in his throat. The three stood still as rocks until the spirit had slowly vanished. Even then they waited, listening to the hiss of falling snow and to the warning of a distant magpie.

Then they moved forward, shadow-silent, each

placing his feet in the other's footprints, breathing lightly and slowly as they followed the vanishing track.

5

Dark fell like sleep over the land. Only the snowflakes shone and shimmered as they sank out of the dark into the glowing coals.

Hunched before the fire, Bright sat like a snow-crowned hillock. Her world had shrunk to the circumference of red light, a tiny point in a cold black universe. What might be going on out there in the dark did not concern Bright.

When she felt a very slight tremor in the earth she recognized the steady rhythm of the men's tread. She raised her head and watched them loom out of the darkness and stand before her in the ruddy light.

The two faces which silently greeted her were identical. Provider and Bisonhorn were twins. Their eyes were the brown of Lefthand's eyes, but they were not anxious or brooding. They were calm impassive eyes set close together above craggy noses and gray-speckled beards. Each twin held a white hare gripped like a club in his hand.

Murmuring happily, Bright wrapped her unconscious baby away from their cold gaze, and stowed it again in her cloak. She asked no questions, but rose eagerly to skin the hares, spit them on sticks, and thrust them into the coals. The innards were gone — the men's color told where — but here was a bite of meat for everyone and two skins. Light like youth came into her face as she worked.

The men sat down by the fire. They yawned, pushed off their boots, and stretched their toes to the warmth. They had hunted far and all day for those two hares which had bounded up before them just at dusk. Two little hares might not seem much reward for a cold day's tramp, but the men were satisfied. This bite would keep them till they found the south-moving herd they expected.

This was the time of year when most creatures turned south. There was a river valley toward which men drifted as the summer sun faded. Now that snow flew, the drift would become a rush, a stampede. From all the northern hills would come the teetering tents, raised each day closer to the valley.

Several winters had passed and Jay had grown from

a toddler to a lanky child while the twins hunted too far west to attempt the journey. This winter they hoped to arrive at the river valley on time. Nothing had been said about this hope. It did not ruffle the frozen waters of their minds. But it was there, swimming below the surface, and it kept their faces turned southeast day after day with few stops or detours.

Tomorrow they would move south again, maybe find a bigger quarry during the day's march. Supper tonight, dinner tomorrow. So let the fire whistle, the blackening meat sizzle and curl. The men wiggled their toes and their noses, inhaling delight.

Gradually they noticed the stillness of the camp: the silent tents, untrodden snow. Provider asked, "Where are the boys?"

"Hunting."

Silence. The twins thought, but no trace of thought appeared on their faces. Because they were inarticulate they thought in pictures, much as did the animals they hunted. In the twins' minds the pictures were practically identical. They each saw three boys trotting tiredly through a snowstorm. The boys were empty-handed. They had dropped their spears far back on the trail and forgotten them. Too weary to press on, they stood huddled together. Hares sprang up around them, birds fluttered about their heads, mice darted between their feet, but the boys were too slow to catch any of these morsels. Now they were jabbering together, pointing north, south, southeast. They were obviously lost.

At this point the pictures differed. Bisonhorn saw his son Onedeer leap on a scuttling rat and catch it! Onedeer had caught a hare bare-handed. He had killed a small deer last summer, jumping at it from ambush with a stone ax in his hand. Bisonhorn grinned to himself. With Onedeer along, the boys would not starve.

Provider's mental picture was less hopeful. He saw the three boys sitting in the snow — the final stupidity — with his promising little son cuddled between the two louts. Inwardly he groaned. Lefthand could sit there and freeze; Provider did not care about him. Since he had learned to walk, Lefthand had done nothing right.

One ability Lefthand did have. In his left hand he had magic that sometimes worked powerfully. Other times it failed. Provider had little patience for magical experiments — he needed results. If Lefthand got himself lost, Provider would not bother to chase after him.

Jay was another matter! Provider had no intention of losing him. He saw himself tramping the country in the first morning light, calling and searching. There would be no trail. Provider sighed.

Bright turned the spits. The smell of roasting meat was now rich and hot and the men leaned toward it, breathing in the aroma of life. Bright lifted her head and shook away the melting snow. She smiled.

The men watched her cracked, worn face soften, and then they heard what she heard.

Out in the dark a voice was talking. Whining, boasting, it came steadily nearer. Inside Bright's cloak the baby also heard the voice and began feebly crying.

Out of the dark came Lefthand, striding manfully. His eyes snapped, his cheeks were red. Jay stumbled after him and went straight to Bright as a hunter goes to his fire. On his half-size spear hung a small stiff shape covered with blood and snow.

"I killed it!" he boasted, and flung it at Bright, "before we saw the spirit! That spirit led us so far, I thought we were lost!"

A faint light, almost like interest, came over the twins' stolid faces.

"What spirit?" Bisonhorn asked Onedeer, as he came last to the fire.

But honest Onedeer looked at Lefthand. It was *his* story!

Lefthand raised his arms, commanding attention.

He stood straight and quiet, looking around at them all until he was sure they were watching. In the shifting firelight he looked tall and earnest — grown up.

Hunching his shoulders, Lefthand rested his hands on his knees. He held his head low, swinging it from side to side, and circled the fire. The men murmured as they understood. Bright pressed Jay against her but he wriggled free and jumped into the act.

Jay gripped his spear, looked excitedly around, and followed exactly in Lefthand's tracks. Around the fire went spirit and following hunter.

Lefthand stopped. Jay stopped. Lefthand stood straight, pranced a step, and spread his fingers above his forehead. Quickly he and Jay trotted around the fire again, heads high, fingers branched, snuffling and snorting.

Now the men were on their feet, excitement shining in their eyes.

"Did you get one?"

"Where is it?"

"How far?"

Proudly Lefthand faced them. He waited till the babble died, then spoke softly into the listening silence.

"The spirit showed us the herd and we will show you. We can catch up with it tomorrow."

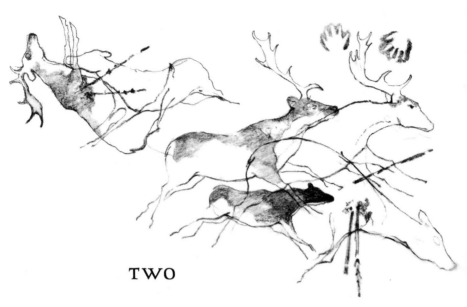

TWO

THE MOON

1

MOONLIGHT SHONE on snow, shone on the outline Lefthand drew in the snow. He sat on his heels,
bent over nose to snow. Clenching his teeth on his
tongue in concentration, he drew with a bone blade
one shaky line after another.

With slow care he drew a forehead sloping to an
open mouth. Bare to the icy night, his mittenless hand
rose in air and traced back up the forehead to draw a
leaf-shaped ear, a round eye. In the glorious haze
through which he saw the drawing this eye appeared
startled, terror-sparked.

With two quick parallel lines he indicated the body.
Two straight lines, one at each end, were the legs. And
a sudden quirk made a tail.

Lefthand crouched over the drawing and con-
sidered. Even in his state of trembling exaltation he
could see that something was wrong. It was not an
animal there, it was a collection of lines. There was
little magic in it. Maybe if he tried harder he could
strengthen the magic which, hunger told him, could
not be too strong.

The head was good, the ear, the frightened eye, but
the body was too straight. With a curving line he
deepened the belly, then added a hump to the back,
just before the tail.

Now he saw. It was the legs! Those two straight
lines — with an impatient stroke he wiped them out.
"Not so fast," he muttered to himself, sweating as he
drew, "think about it . . . front legs bend forward,
like this . . . hind legs back . . . the heel sticks out
so . . . " He raised his hand and sat back. Magic rose
from the drawing like a spring from the ground.

The deer drawn in the moonlit snow was young.
His slender neck, the delicate lines of his legs and, of
course, the lack of antlers showed that he was only a
fawn. Beautiful he was and very lifelike, but there was
barely enough meat on him to feed a fox.

The artist's all-powerful hand hung poised over the fawn, ready to wipe him out of existence. But Lefthand hesitated. He saw that it was not necessary to destroy the fawn. He could make him grow.

Experimentally he thickened the neck and shoulder. Good. He added a mane and a bulge of muscle to the hind leg. Good. Nervously fingering his bone blade, he bowed solemnly to the final touch — the antlers.

Two forked sticks were attached to the head. Mumbling under his breath, Lefthand hastily swatted them away. He shut his eyes, trying to visualize antlers. The mental image swam and blended; he could not get a clear look. He was too conscious of the moon moving up the sky, and the impatient sighs of those around him.

He opened his eyes and there on the snow, a step from his nose, stood antler shadows! There was the image in clear black and white. Into his eyes flowed the antler shape, powerfully it streamed from eye to hand, from hand to snow. There galloped a finished reindeer, legs flexed, eye alert, strongly crowned.

Lefthand sank back on his heels and looked at it. His heart expanded. He felt it stretching inside him to fill his chest. Its beat thundered in his ears and he breathed hard in the grip of joy.

It was the same feeling he had when he made a spearhead, carefully chipping the bone, holding his breath as he shaped the tip. The moment came when the spearhead was finished, when he could hold it in his hand, heft it, know that it was really a part of himself, yet outside himself, a bit of Lefthand firmly imposed on the outside vastness. The best moment came when Provider lifted the spearhead, weighed it in his hand, and nodded satisfaction. If it pleased Provider — if it pleased anyone, even Onedeer — it was real. It was born like a baby, out of dream into reality.

Now Lefthand unwillingly tore his delighted gaze from the drawing. He looked at the shadow antlers, swaying slightly across the sketch from him. His eyes followed the shadow back to the deerskin boots, standing positive and straddled, up the stocky legs to the worn jacket, and Provider's considering face.

The twins stood together, spears in hand. They were wrapped in reindeer skins whose antlers branched over their heads. The tattered reindeer foreheads fell to their eyes, which hungrily dwelt on the magic drawing. Onedeer stood back to the side. His fair, handsome face was sulky.

Provider bent down to examine the sketch. He looked at it upside down and walked around to see it right side up. He squatted before it and raised a questioning face to his brother.

"Yes," Bisonhorn nodded.

Lefthand clasped his arms and squeezed himself. He felt he might burst like a seedpod, and let out joy.

Provider took the small bone blade that hung from his waist and set the point to his thumb. He pressed and the dent in the skin became a hole. Black in the moonlight, a drop of blood oozed out of the hole. Provider leaned over the drawing and shook his thumb, and blood spattered the reindeer's head. Serious and silent, Bisonhorn was pricking his own thumb. Then Onedeer came forward into the circle, blade at the ready.

Lefthand hastened to snatch up his own blade and press the point to his own thumb. He scarcely felt it and he managed to keep a grave, noncommittal face like Provider's, as he too shook blood onto his drawing.

Now the hunters struck their spears into the snow and crouched beside Lefthand. Opening their right hands wide, they pressed the palms all around the reindeer, one here, one there, until the palm prints looked like the track of some weird monster stalking the deer. Turn where he would, the sketched deer could not escape; he would trot straight into the printed hands.

Provider indicated that one thing remained to be done. He waved his spear so that its shadow fell across the deer. Hastily, Lefthand drew four straight lines rammed into the deer's throat, chest, stomach, and rump.

This broke the flow of the lines, and Lefthand forgot the intense joy he had felt in them. Indifferent now, he stood up with the hunters and moved away, leaving the moon to watch over the drawing.

Later in the night a mouse scrambled across and erased it.

2

Moonlight shone on the herd in the hollow. Antlers gleamed in the white light. Held high, held low, swinging, bobbing antlers forested the mossy gorge. A constant clicking troubled the air, the click of antlers and hoofs and bony joints. Reindeer browsed and scraped the snow and slept, for as far as the fawn could see.

The fawn was used to being in the center of the herd, fenced in by countless slender legs, smelling milk and moss and deer. Here on the edge of the herd he was drowned in a sea of new perceptions. The world went on by itself, bare of legs or antlers. The cold wind smelled only incidentally of moss; there were other mingled scents that wrinkled his nose.

Before him arose the ice-sprayed rock of the gorge wall, twice as high as his head. Junipers looked down over its edge and beyond it hung the moon. Over the gorge wall whined a chill wind, bearing unfamiliar smells that drifted down to the fawn's expanding nostrils. Two of these smells were very unpleasant. One was quite close, the other faint and farther away. Neither raised any picture in the fawn's mind. He snorted to clear his nose. Then he capered back to his mother who lay content in a soft snow bed, chewing her cud and watching him.

Lefthand also watched him. Crouched in the junipers on top of the gorge wall, he saw the fawn walk over and stand beneath him, flicking its tail and looking about with wide dark eyes. He saw it test the air, he saw its surprised look. His heart stood still but the fawn looked up and past him with a large, wondering gaze. Then it snorted, jumped, and bucked, and bolted back to the doe.

Lefthand watched it with excitement. It was the fawn he had sketched back in the forest glade. Surely it was the same deer! He was not really surprised for he knew he had this magic. He turned from the fawn and looked away down the gorge into the forest of antlers and haunches. The sight of so much meat so close awakened hunger in him as pain. If he closed his eyes now, he would see in the dark of his brain a fading fire, a crackling reindeer shoulder . . .

Would the wolf never call?

Lefthand glanced across to the opposite bank of the narrow gorge only ten strides wide. Immediately his eyes met the ravenous eyes of Onedeer, peering wolfishly through the junipers.

Then Lefthand remembered. Had the fawn sensed his urgency. He made himself relax and sat limp, listening to the cough and click of the herd.

The doe lurched to her feet. Head up, nose wrinkling, she looked straight at Lefthand. . . . No, she was looking beyond him.

Far down at the south end of the gorge a wolf howled.

Lefthand's eyes met Onedeer's, and a thought flashed between them. It might be a real wolf!

The reindeer were lifting their heads, testing the air. The doe stamped, still looking over Lefthand's head. The wolf howled again, this time with an exasperated note.

Together the boys rose. Shouting like night fiends they hurled their spears.

They were to frighten and stampede the herd toward the waiting men. Lefthand did not take time to aim carefully, and was not surprised to see his spear dive into the snow a good pace behind his fawn's rump. He had thrown at the fawn because he had a magical connection with it. The doe would have been a better target, but now it was too late to think of that. He was leaping from the bank, and running to retrieve his spear.

A young buck trotted dazedly past him. In its plump side bobbed a spear with blood welling and running around the shaft. Onedeer had aimed with care. The buck would fall before the men ever touched it. It would be Onedeer's second kill.

Now the fawn was again in the midst of the herd, pushed and jostled by shoulders and antlers. Through the milling legs two weird figures ran toward him, sticks flying ahead. His mother pushed against him, almost knocking him down, but he was pushed again from the other side. Now the herd was running. Earth rumbled, snow flew up from a hundred churning hoofs. The fawn could not see where he ran. He followed the white rump ahead and ran from the howls behind.

The pursuers felt the rumble of the galloping herd in their feet. In their bodies they felt the pulse of hunger, of their own pounding blood. They ran in a great, feeling noise.

Halfway down the gorge the running herd left behind a dark shape on the snow. Onedeer's buck writhed on his side, his short antlers scraping snow and earth. Onedeer paused to wrench out his spear. Lefthand jumped over the buck and ran on.

The fawn rammed into the deer ahead. The herd had suddenly stopped. Sharp hoofs trod on his back, knocking him to the ground. Through the forest of legs he saw new terrors approaching, two creatures, antlered, smelling strangely of deer. A stick flew and dug into the shoulder of the big buck ahead. The buck sagged. The herd divided and flowed around him and between the two fearsome shapes. The fawn struggled to his feet and bolted blindly forward.

[41]

Provider's spear whizzed over the fawn's back, and struck the doe beyond. The fawn rushed out of the gorge into wide, moonlit space.

3

Moonlight shone on trampled snow; on blood-soaked moss; on the eager, wildly happy people moving among the kills.

Lefthand stood gulping two handfuls of innards. Warm blood trickled between his fingers and he licked them.

Bright crouched over a carcass, pulling back the skin with her hands and a bone blade. In the moonlight her hair shone white, her hands blood-black. Onedeer came and gave her a pile of innards cupped in his hands. Jay hopped up and stood looking greedily.

Bright gave Jay the pile, of course, and licked the blood from her hands while the child laughed and ate and laughed again, jumping like a wolf puppy around the carcass. Lefthand laughed, gurgling through his mouthful, and Onedeer ran back to help the men cut out more innards.

Lefthand stood idle. He had not killed a single animal and so could not split any stomach or hand out the steaming riches within. He could help Bright with the skinning. Maybe later he would, but not now while the others were gleefully gutting their kills.

He looked around for Onedeer's buck. It lay fifty paces back in the shadow of the bank. It could have been a rock or a mound of moss, but for the white belly faintly reflecting moonlight.

Lefthand went slowly back to it. He stooped, blade in hand. The air around was heavy with blood-scent, the aroma of spilled life. Only this buck lay intact, unopened, its vitals writhing in secret under the skin. Lefthand was tempted. His hand reached out with the blade — and stopped. He had no right.

He turned and opened his mouth to call Onedeer. "Come gut your buck!"

Bright was looking at him. Her eyes were two immense holes of darkness, her mouth a third.

Jay froze in mid-leap. He came to earth in a crouch, and grabbed Bright's arm. His mouth hung blackly open.

Farther back the three hunters stood together. They stared, guts oozing unnoticed through their

[43]

fingers. Onedeer pointed. His finger was aimed beyond Lefthand, just as the doe had looked beyond
him.

Lefthand had time to engrave this picture on his
mind before he was seized.

4

Tremendous claws raked his chest and stomach.
Wounds burned his flesh. One, two, three flashes of
pain, and he stopped feeling.

His open eyes continued to see. The hands that
held and ripped him were black in the moonlight.
They were hairy, strong with the strength of three
men. He knew then who held him, whose furious
growl tunneled through his head.

Would the men move?

They stood like rocks, popeyed, slack-jawed. They
were not afraid of animals. But this enemy was not
entirely animal.

It was Bright who moved. Shrilly screaming, she
leaped up. Spreading her fingers like claws, she

bounded forward. She was unarmed and had even dropped her bone blade, but her crooked, bloody fingers, her streaming hair, and the agony of anger that gnarled her face gave the bear pause.

He thrust his long snout across Lefthand's shoulder and snarled at Bright.

Past the fanged jaw that jutted against his cheek, Lefthand saw Jay spring up. He did not believe it, but he saw Jay snatch a severed antler and run, yelling, *toward* him.

Lefthand felt himself lifted, dragged back. One monster hand held him, the other reached over his shoulder grabbing at Bright and Jay. They hopped like hares, screaming, raking the air with fingers and antler.

And now at last the hunters moved. Through a deepening red mist Lefthand saw them run up. They held their spears backward so as not to injure their spirit friend, but hold the spears they did, and jab and poke, while the claws swatted and the woman and child leaped around them. The air was rent with screams, grunts, and growls. Sometimes the spear butts jabbed Lefthand, but mostly they thudded against the sides and legs of the bear.

Provider worked around to the side and delivered a telling blow. Lefthand felt himself released and dropped. The hairy, long-clawed spirit foot whose track he had followed stood directly before his eyes, planted like an oak. Then it rose in air and withdrew. A deerskin boot planted itself on the spot like a slender sapling. Moonlight and shadow mingled and swam in the thickening red mist.

THREE

THE DARK

1

FAR THROUGH THE MOONLIGHT ran the fawn. His long legs pumped steadily, strongly. His heart thumped a regular loud rhythm. All his being was action. His senses were numb to the whiteness around him, snow-white and moon-white, to the click and pant of other deer running near him. His brain was filled with the image of the two fearsome figures, the antlered monsters. His ears still carried their howls, his nostrils their scent.

The fawn ran more slowly as his heartbeat became a

painful thud. He gasped for air in harsh, aching breaths. He stumbled and finally stopped. His brain stirred and woke from nightmare.

Around him was white silence. He twitched his ears and caught no sound but familiar deer noises and those were at a distance. Lifting his head with an effort he spread his nostrils and found no whiff of the monster-scent. The fawn began to look around.

The herd had scattered over a wide, tumbled slope. Bushes and young trees blocked the fawn's view, but after gazing a while in the direction of a wheezing sound he caught sight of a large gray shape obscured behind a willow clump. The shape flicked its tail, a small bright flash in shadow, and the fawn made a weak leap of joy.

He swung around and headed in stumbling haste for the willows. Already in anticipation he felt the doe's rough tongue kissing his shoulder, he tasted her warm milk. Eagerly he staggered away from loneliness, closer to the gray form.

It was not the doe. The fawn knew that before he came around the willows. He stood downcast, looking after the panting deer who moved slowly away. He was an old buck whose heavy antlers and snowy ruff dwarfed his bony hindquarters. He paused and looked

[48]

back at the fawn. His eyes were startled at first, then mildly friendly. He turned away and continued his slow progress along the slope, and the fawn followed. He could not remain alone.

Through the bushes went the unlikely pair, brushing the branches, snatching at winter-tight buds. Other shapes appeared, stepping out from thickets and hollows of darkness. Slowly the herd was coming together, finding itself, moving always along the hillside away from the sinking moon.

The fawn smelled each new arrival hopefully. He would dart forward at sight of an adult herd member, then stop in his tracks and look mournfully around for another. The deer smell was overwhelming around him. But still he looked and smelled for the one at whose side he had always walked and browsed and slept.

When the exhausted reindeer let themselves down in the snow to rest, the fawn lay down by himself, alone in his own skin. There was no warm flank to snuggle against, no moss-scented breath meeting his own. He turned on his side and stretched, reaching out his nose and tail and the tips of his hoofs. A sharp pain ripped across his stomach. The fawn threw up his head and gathered his feet to rise. The pain became intense and steady and he could not rise because of something wrapped around him.

He opened his eyes wide with fear in the fading gray moonlight and wondered.

And then he thought, "What am I doing here!"

Now Lefthand remembered himself. He was not a reindeer fawn. He had no tired, heavy hoofs. His feet were encased in stiff boots and lay side by side as though he were dead. The running, the search for the doe, the gathering herd — he had dreamed all that. This was reality: darkness, pain, a thick warm skin wrapped firmly around him, and a loneliness colder than that of the orphan fawn.

The young reindeer had strong, swift legs. His eyes and ears and nose were competent. He needed the doe only for comfort and kindness.

Lefthand had no strength. He knew that he had sustained some terrible injury. Now he remembered what had happened. Staring into blankness, he saw again the hideous, grinning jaw thrust past his cheek, and the reaching, swatting paw with its long curving claws. Lefthand sweated under the robe. He remembered his father, and Bisonhorn and Onedeer, standing and watching while the bear grabbed him.

Had they gone away now and left him? He could easily imagine their doing it. No words would be spoken. His father Provider would make a gesture, a spread hand with the palm down, and the others would bundle up the meat in the skins and walk away. Bright would wrap the robe about him first, a final gift, and Jay would look back and whisper, "Why?"

Straining his ears, Lefthand heard no sound. Spreading his nostrils almost as the fawn had done, he caught a wonderful scent — a whiff of woodsmoke.

Very slowly, neck muscles bulging, Lefthand turned his head. Away to his right the dimness was touched with red. If he turned a little farther . . . He moved his shoulders and pain woke all up and down his chest. He had to know. Gritting his teeth, he turned his head as far as possible till he was looking flat along the snow.

A red glow framed a huddled shape.

Lefthand breathed a deep sigh of relief. He knew that shape, that scene. From his infancy, darkness, red glow, slumping silhouette, had been the form of Home. Waking at night as a little child, loved and fed and not expected to hunt, he had seen a woman hunched beside her dozing fire.

And now he sensed the presence of other sleepers. Curled in their skin robes they sighed and stirred, giving off reassuring smells of woodsmoke, blood, and sweat.

Lefthand lay looking steadily at the comforting shape outlined in red. His head swam with pain and he wondered vaguely if it might not all be a dream. He was not a fawn. Perhaps he was not a wounded young hunter either. Perhaps he would wake in the morning and find himself a dark, dreamy little boy already called Lefthand. He would get up hungry, and Mother would gladly find him a bit of meat she had hidden among her jumbled possessions on the baggage sled. He would take his little spear and hurl it at trees and if he missed it would not matter. He would wrestle with Onedeer and Onedeer would win, and that wouldn't matter either. Comforted by this confused hope he let his eyelids sink, and darkness came.

Behind Bright the sky gradually lightened until the sun rose, small and cold, in the wide winter sky. Morning shone into the camp and the hunters moaned to themselves. They pulled their robes over their faces and turned away from the light. They had marched all the day before and hunted all the night. They had eaten and now their stomachs were deliciously full, their robes were warm, and daylight could not arouse them.

Lefthand lay unconscious, drowned in a rising tide of fever. Jay opened one eye, looked at the morning, and rolled over tighter in his bison skin. Bright, nodding by the fire, began to dream.

She saw a pair of small, soft hands stringing a necklace. They were the hands of a little girl named Bright. She was stringing reindeer vertebrae on a cord of twisted sinew. Some of the hollow bones were painted red, some black, some with red or black dots. The stubby little hands worked patiently and Bright felt a throb of joy in the beauty of the growing necklace.

But wait! What was this? The biggest vertebra, red, with black specks — the one to go in the middle — was broken. The small hands held it up and turned it around, and Bright saw how hopelessly destroyed it was. Some heavy boot had trampled and crushed it. She began to cry. For the first time in many years Bright felt tears welling into her eyes and spilling down her cheeks. Her vision of the necklace was blurred.

"What's the matter, Bright?" A voice spoke in her ear. She did not need to look because she knew the voice. Her father was standing over her, bent and crooked. His gentle smile showed all his broken teeth.

"Let me see," he urged, and she held up her little hands and showed him in one hand the necklace, in the other the smashed bone.

"Hmmm," she heard him mumbling to himself. "Where did you get it?"

"My sister," she heard herself say.

"But your sister hasn't been born."

Bright turned her head and looked up at her father bent crookedly beside her shoulder. Yellow hair streaked with gray stuck stiffly out from his head. His teeth gleamed in a smile which resembled a savage snarl. His keen blue eyes held her gaze steady. Once having looked into his eyes she could not look away.

"Never mind," he said, "give it to me. Give it to me." He held out a gnarled hand for the necklace. Just then Bright heard a miserable, whining noise and her father faded away into daylight.

The whining was persistent and there was a crawling motion in her cloak. Her baby. Wide awake now, Bright lifted it out of its dark nest and turned its wizened face to the light. "Day," she murmured to it, "see, it's day!"

At any moment the baby would break into its sick screaming. She had better take it away from the camp before it disturbed the sleepers. Squinting into the morning, Bright heaved herself up and carried the whimpering baby away. She noticed the dying fire as she went, and the stiffly crumpled bundle that was Lefthand. She shook her head and mumbled.

Later in the morning she returned with an unconscious baby and an armload of wood. Squatting, she fed her fire stick by stick until the flames leaped up to greet the sun. The men would not stir till noon. She would have time to peg out a slippery new skin and scrape it and talk to herself. But first she went and stood over Lefthand.

She bent down and examined his deeply flushed face and listened to his harsh breathing. Her mild, good-natured expression turned sorrowfully hard.

2

Embers glowed through gray, slow-rolling mist. Over the embers hovered a thick stooping figure. It squatted and reached for twigs. Clothed in pain, Lefthand squinted and with a great effort he murmured. The figure straightened and turned toward him, letting the twigs fall. It came to him, extending kind hands, and it was Bright.

She laid a rough, fire-hot hand on his cheek, then on his forehead She went away out of his small world and came back with a handful of damp moss. This she patted onto his forehead and over his eyes, and in the dark he felt the icy relief of snow being heaped on the moss.

Much later he opened his aching eyes on the gray mist and saw Bright sitting near him, bent over, intent. Silently wrapped in his own pain, he watched for some time the still, tiny form in her lap. Oblivious to Lefthand and his needs she breathed warmth onto the baby, tenderly stroked it, laid a hand on its palm-sized chest, and listened at its mouth. At last she wrapped it tightly in its hare skin, rose heavily, and carried it away.

Lefthand stifled a moan of fury. He needed that hare skin to warm his numb feet. Bright had used it to warm the dead.

As the pain and fever gradually subsided and the gray mist rolled farther back, Lefthand came to hate Bright. He hated her carefully gentle touch and the soft look she bent upon him, the same she had given her useless infant. As she had cared for that baby, shielding it from the men's indifference, so she now cared for him. Sometimes Lefthand saw a dim masculine form, obscure in mist, looking at him over Bright's shoulder. It would stand tall, not bothering to lean toward him. It would look at him in silence and move away.

[56]

Once a silent observer leaned over to see him closer. Then it stepped up and crouched beside him. It reached out a hand and lightly touched his shoulder.

"Aaaarch!" Lefthand snarled, as pain leaped along his nerves.

Hastily the hand lifted off but the face was still there. Onedeer's blue eyes looked hopefully into his.

Onedeer spoke quickly, softly. "Get up," he said, "you must try to get up, Lefthand. We can't stay here much longer."

Bright pushed Onedeer aside. Her large hand came down like night over Lefthand's eyes. He heard her angry grunt.

Faintly, from a distance he heard Onedeer's help-less question and saw Bright turn away.

Swimming halfheartedly in his lake of pain, Left-hand dreamed of hunting. He was crawling through high grass toward a sound of chomping. Just ahead he saw a tail swish among the grasses; he was after a pony. Softly now, softly, he grasped his spear and began to rise. Pain struck like lightning.

Wakened by the pain, which was real, he lay hope-less. He did not know why Bright insisted on cleaning him up as best she could and feeding him. She brought him burned and pre-chewed meat which he washed down with handfuls of snow. Why could she not leave him to sink into his private world of pain, and through it to snowy silence?

Silence was unnatural to Bright. When she saw Lefthand awake, she talked. When he wanted nothing but to listen to a moaning wind or the howl of a distant wolf, words tumbled into his ears.

"This skin is soft enough to make Jay a new jacket. Feel it, Lefthand! The deer must not have been a year old. Feel the fuzz! Now, what does Jay need more, a jacket or a pair of mittens?"

Lefthand could have told her that he himself needed an entire new outfit. His clothes, stuck to his wounds with his own dried blood, stank. But he would not ask her for anything and tempt that hateful soft look to come into her face. Worse still, he was afraid. He did not like to imagine his wounds uncovered.

She would sometimes laugh suddenly, breaking blessed silence, and tell him a story. "Did I ever tell you about the time I made a snow boar?"

Lefthand opened his eyes and squinted at her, half interested. Encouraged, she went on. "I was a little girl then, you know, and nobody ever told me that there was magic in pretend things. It was just a game. Well, I made a beautiful boar out of snow. He stood as high as this, believe it or not, and he had icicle tusks. And just as I was finishing him, putting on the tail like this" — pat pat pat — "I heard an awful noise — *Rrrraugh!* — and I looked around." Bright swung toward him, surprisingly agile. "And what do you think I saw, Lefthand?"

Lefthand forced himself to speak. It still hurt to make a voice. "A boar?"

"Yes, that's right. He was coming at me out of a thicket like this." Bright lowered her head and snarled, baring her yellow teeth. Wickedness gleamed in her eyes as she stormed clumsily around the fire. Lefthand smiled.

"Who killed him?" he asked.

Bright stopped being the boar. She stood looking at Lefthand as though waking from a dream. "Who killed him? Why . . . nobody. There was nobody around who could. You know my father couldn't kill a boar!"

"So, what did you do?"

"I jumped up in the nearest oak, that's what I did. And the boar rooted and roared around for a while, and then he . . . went off." Bright laughed gently, remembering. "And the first thing I did when I came down from the tree, I knocked down that snow boar!"

Lefthand sighed. He wished she would let him sleep. All her stories were pointless.

Another time she said, "When we get there, I will take you to my father."

In Lefthand's misty mind an image formed, firmed, brightened. A tall figure stamped and swayed in strong sunlight. About its legs hung a spirit robe of heavy fur. Antlers like trees rose from its brow and giant claws flopped and flipped from its fingers.

"The Bear!" he cried. He tried to rise but pain gripped his belly.

Bright pushed him gently down.

"Yes," she said. "My father is sometimes like a bear. That is why he can cure you." Lefthand looked away from her. Despair must be plain on his face and he did not want her to see it. She added encouragingly, "But most of the time, he is like a squirrel."

The memory of the Bear led into another. Lefthand was young like Jay. He was standing trembling in a strange place full of terrifying noise. Other children ran about, shouting and leaping, like quick shadows against a brilliant sky. One of them came swooping toward him, arms outstretched like a fluttering bird. Very clearly he saw a small, brown face close to his own. A little girl stood before him, hopefully friendly, ready to smile.

[60]

"Snowbird," he said, dreamily.

"Oh yes," said Bright, "my sister."

The next day Lefthand sat up. Bright and Jay helped him, pushing at his elbows, pulling at his shoulders till he was sitting against a fir trunk, his knees folded to his chest, holding in the pain. He sat there groggily for a while, supporting himself with both hands flat on the ground. When he opened his eyes he saw Onedeer sitting across the fire.

Onedeer had changed. For a moment Lefthand was not sure it was he. It was a young man, not a child, sitting there and working at something on his knees. His face was earnest, his hands large and skillful. Lefthand saw a new softness on his lip and chin — the first hint of a blond beard.

Onedeer smiled at Lefthand. With both hands he raised the thing he was doing so Lefthand could see it above the cloud of smoke between them.

It was a reindeer mask. Onedeer had hollowed out the head of his buck. The eyes were ragged holes and the mouth drooped, lopsided, beneath the heavy antlers. Gravely Onedeer lowered the mask over his own head and tilted his head back and sideways to look through the eye holes at Lefthand.

Lefthand tried to smile but he felt a cold, lonely

sorrow. He felt as though Onedeer had walked away from him over a hilltop and for several nights he dreamed of the deer mask mockingly tilting its antlers.

Onedeer came to Lefthand once more because Bright had called him. Lefthand watched them confer with vigorous gestures. Bright wanted to do something and Onedeer was certain it could not be done. He pointed at Lefthand, pressed his own chest with both hands and contorted his face into a mask of anguish.

Onedeer was fast becoming a man, a hunter, who lived only by signs and facts. But Bright lived by faith. Her faith won. Onedeer shrugged and gave in. He came over to Lefthand, smiled an impersonal greeting, and seized him by the shoulders. At the same moment Bright grabbed his feet. Lefthand snatched a breath and held it and did not scream. Onedeer and Bright worked fast and roughly, and Lefthand was sure he was dying. They rolled him over, face to snow, face to sky, face to a strange surface.

Gasping, he recognized it. He was lying on the baggage sled. Boots stood around him: Bright's, worn almost past usefulness, Onedeer's, soft and new, and a small new pair.

"Lefthand!" Jay squeaked above him, "Lefthand, you're coming with us!"

Lefthand moaned a half-conscious answer. At the same time the sled jerked into motion. Crumpled on top of Bright's skins and tools and three reindeer masks, Lefthand drifted into a stupor.

An agonizing jolt woke him. The baggage sled had hit a jutting tree root. Even as Lefthand gasped and his eyes flew open, the sled swerved and hit another. He clutched the birch frame to steady himself.

Under his nose jerked a snowy landscape. Face to snow he saw the world as mice see it. Roots loomed large. Footprints were valleys. Dead grass and bushes reared like trees.

They were moving steadily uphill. Lefthand was dreamily aware that they had been climbing for some time. It would hurt to try to look in front, and if he did, he would see only Bright's broad back bowed to his weight, and her boots patiently denting the snow.

He heard a thudding behind them. Carefully, Lefthand peered over the rim of the sled and saw Jaybird was pounding up the slope, jumping from root to root and by dint of giant strides setting his feet in Bright's tracks. In one mittened hand he waved something dark and fuzzy. He was almost up to the sled before Lefthand saw it was a ptarmigan, held by the feet. The open beak still dripped blood, spattering the snow.

[63]

"I got it!" Jay shrilled, catching hold of the sled to steady himself.

Bright growled at the extra weight. Lefthand winced at the jerk of the sled. Jay dumped his ptarmigan abruptly onto Lefthand's back and ran forward, squealing, "I got us a bird!"

Very gently, Lefthand tried to squirm around and dislodge the corpse. He was still carefully wiggling when a squeak sounded ahead. "Oooeee!"

They stopped moving. The sled stood on level ground. Looking around, Lefthand saw five pairs of boots standing about him. The twins had joined them. Everyone was there, together, looking ahead.

Lefthand felt a strange thrill, a beat in his blood. Slowly he realized that it came through his ears. He was hearing the earth's heartbeat and it spoke to him. From deep inside he felt a response, an unwilling answer.

Till this moment Lefthand had felt himself dead. Now he knew he was alive, that there was something to want, something to reach for. In a little while he would remember what it was.

Weakly he gripped the birch rim of the sled under his chin. His hands, white-knuckled and shaking, could still grasp. Then he began to rise to his knees. The hurt was there, screaming inside him, but Lefthand did not listen to it. The great outside heartbeat sounded louder in his ears.

Now he was on hands and knees, weakly wavering. He might have crumpled but strong hands slipped under his waist. They hurt, but they supported him and slowly Lefthand crept up the strong tree that was Bright. Standing, the rhythmic thunder booming through him, he pushed away from her and turned around.

Directly before him earth fell away. Sky spread forward.

3

Lefthand looked down through intense brightness and saw a wide valley stretched below. Through its center coiled a river white with ice. On either side flat snowfields reached to the bases of mountains. Across the valley, the mountains reared, brown and green, cave-pitted, white with snow and gray with sheer cliffs.

Brown patches broke the snowfields. One was a herd of animals. As he watched it moved, weaving slowly about itself. The brown patches close beneath him were tents, a hundred or more which stood and leaned in a wide arc crowded together like a herd of bison. From there came the throbbing, the heartbeat.

Encircled by the arc of tents and smoky fires a huge, fantastic herd cavorted. He could clearly see the tossing horns and swishing tails of black, brown, and red creatures who stamped and jumped to the drumbeat.

Around the herd, among the fires, moved vigorous human forms. Children raced and leaped over fires and wrestled in the snow beyond. Women stooped over meat racks, turning strips of meat in the smoke. Some, looking like piles of walking brush, carried wood to the fires. Others stood about in eager groups. Faint through the drum thunder could be heard the roar of countless voices.

Lefthand looked down into the smoky melee and felt his brain open inside his head and spill a vision. This thing that sometimes happened to him, the strange dark thing that he had never talked about, even to Onedeer, had happened again. The bright scene darkened as though a cloud had suddenly crossed the sun. Below him Lefthand saw, not a crowd of happy people, but a deadly pack. The world's most

ferocious and dangerous creatures were gathered together under the cliff in riotous glee. Every man dancing under his horned mask in the magic circle was a
successful killer of large animals, creatures five and ten
times his own weight. Without claws or horns or
biting fangs, he killed constantly, using his brain to
devise weapons and his clever hands to make them.
He brought down galloping ponies, for he could send
his spear flying faster than he could run, as quick as
his thought. Every man in that pounding dance was a
terror, a threat to the rest of existence. The drum said
so, the postures of the dancers said so.

Lefthand had always known this and had taken
pride in it. Now he saw the threat in a new light, from
a revealing height. He saw that these predators might
be dangerous even to each other.

Lefthand had never seen one human actively, deliberately, injure another. He had never heard of such
a thing, but he saw in this flash of evil vision that it
could happen, it could happen very easily. For the
dancers were hunters — killers.

He felt fear rising like sickness in his throat and he
choked it down. He shook his head violently, shaking
out the vision. Now he saw bright sunlight, a group of
sociable people delighting in each other's company, a

magic dance intended to bring reindeer into the valley — reindeer who could already be seen on the horizon.

Beside Lefthand, Jay let out his breath in a long, unbelieving sigh and said, "Are we going down there?"

"Yes. That is the Meeting Valley."

"How do we get down?"

"There's a path down the cliff."

"Lefthand! How will *you* get down?"

"I will have to walk. You must help me." He would walk like a human into that company, even if it killed him. He turned to the others.

Onedeer and the twins were crouched in a huddle. They were digging into their dangling pouches. Their hands came out coated red, as if with blood. Wiping their fingers across their faces they left shiny red lines around their eyes and down their cheeks. They looked at each other and chuckled approval. Their mouths loosened and smiled and their eyes widened.

"That's paint," Lefthand told Jay. "It's red earth and fat. Men put it on when they meet people."

Jay at once began squeaking, "Me too, me too!" Lefthand hushed him. "Only men," he said bitterly.

Onedeer stood up. The paint glowed grittily on his cheeks. He went to the baggage sled and lifted the three reindeer masks. The men eased the antlered skins onto their heads and Onedeer solemnly put on his buck's head. He looked once at Lefthand through the paint and mask. Then he looked away.

They were ready to climb down the cliff.

"Lefthand!" Jay slipped a small, timid hand into his brother's. "Stay with me?"

Never had he seen so many people all together or heard such tremendous noise. In their wanderings the family sometimes had met other family bands. For a while they might pitch their tents together and share a season of good hunting. As soon as the animals grew scarce, they would break camp and each family would hunt separately.

They had wandered far since Lefthand was little. His mother had died the last winter they had come to this valley. Most people came every winter but the twins had wandered too far to return. Years had passed since Lefthand had seen this gathering. Jay had never seen it. Feeling Jay trembling against him, Lefthand remembered the stomach-shivering terror that he, as a little boy, had felt here.

Roughly he squeezed the small, seeking hand and reminded him, "I'll have to stay with you, Jay! I can't even walk!"

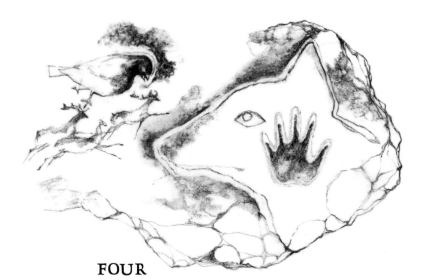

FOUR

THE VALLEY

1

AS A MOUNTAIN STREAM LEAPS from its last
rocky cleft it broadens, slows, gurgles down toward
the plain to join the broader river. So the little band of
Lefthand's people emerged from the cliff shadow and
fanned slowly out, advancing toward the crowd.

They would never again be all together. As a reindeer senses the unheard hunter in the thicket, so Lefthand guessed the coming breakup of his world. He
could do nothing but push painfully forward with the
others, then behind from them and finally alone with
Jay and Bright.

He would not crawl. He walked, though not erect,

because the lacerations on his chest and stomach were healing in aching lumps. He limped hunched over, resting on Jay's slight shoulder.

Dark quick children darted out of his way. They shot astonished glances at him, then humped themselves up and limped, shaking with laughter. But when they saw Jay their eyes turned friendly.

Women, talking in clusters, moved slightly aside for him and went on talking. From wild hair to their boots, the short, heavy figures were swathed in worn, patched skins. Their hands moved constantly, gesturing at the brilliant sky, at fires, tents, and trodden snow. They shook fists, arched brows, wriggled shoulders, snapped fingers. Eyes black, brown, and blue, shone with the rapture of talk.

Somewhere among these swarming clusters Lefthand lost Bright. He came limping to the inner edge of the crowd, the heart of the drumbeat. It drowned out the women's voices and the children's shrieks. Lefthand felt himself swimming weakly through a river of rhythm that pulsed around and through him, up from his feet and down from his ears. White earth and blue sky shimmered and shook together.

A great circle of earth was trodden bare. Here danced the magic herd. Tireless booted feet rose and fell together, following each other in an endless ring.

With antlers askew, and skin flapping, a reindeer

and then a bison passed. The head waved menacingly, the horns curved out like balancing wings. Under the bison skin stamped four boots. A red wolf loped beside the deer, its needled jaws aimed straight up at the sky. Out of its throat smiled a young, painted face. Two ponies followed, one gray, one shining black. Their tails swished to the drumbeat, their little polished hoofs beat time.

Lefthand lowered himself gingerly to sit on the snow. His eyes stared, his head throbbed. All his wounds ached. At his back he felt Jay squatting, shivering.

The circle broke for an instant. There in the center danced the Bear. It stamped, then bounded into the air and stamped again. Heavy bear fur swung from its shoulders. Bear claws raked the air, a white horsetail swept the snow. On the reindeer head antlers branched high into the sky. From under the fringed deer brow ferocious blue eyes glared straight at Lefthand, who shrank in dread from the look of recognition in those glimmering eyes.

Then he was looking at a pair of slim boots that stood firmly between himself and the dance. He looked up. Snowbird was tall and lean now, but her face was the same warm brown that he remembered; her eyes still smiled. Lefthand felt Jay slowly rising at his back, drawn to her friendliness as a flower is drawn to the sun.

Snowbird crouched in front of Lefthand so that he would not have to look up. She spoke to him, shouting through the drum thunder, as though she had last seen him yesterday.

"My sister told me you were here!" she yelled. "Show me what the bear did!"

Lefthand was silent. He had little practice in instant speech and Snowbird's familiarity startled him.

"He ripped him up the front!" Jay yelled over Lefthand's shoulder.

"Let me see." She put out a hand — small and thin and laced with blue veins — and grasped the edge of Lefthand's jacket. Lefthand watched her face as she tugged at the edge and lifted it away from the ooze underneath. He said nothing and did not flinch, but her eyes widened and she gently patted the garment down flat.

"Yes, it's bad," she said. "You need a new outfit, Lefthand. I will make you one!"

Lefthand opened his mouth at last and made answer. "I need a new body!" he shouted, and Snowbird laughed. Her teeth were strong and white.

The drum stopped. Silence startled them. Jaybird gripped Lefthand's shoulder hard, leaning around him to see into the circle. "Get off!" Lefthand hissed, but Jay was frightened and he held on in panic, as an infant squirrel holds onto the bark of a tree. Snowbird turned to look and Lefthand saw, over her shoulder, that the dance had stopped in mid-step.

In the middle of the circle a reindeer danced around the Bear. He waved his hands frantically, fingers stretched and pointing insistently north. He tossed his head and leaped and skipped, all the time jabbing his antler-miming fingers at the north. The Bear turned around ponderously, keeping his grim face toward the jibbering dancer. The reindeer figure seemed familiar to Lefthand, and as he came around the Bear the third time his mask slipped back from half his face, and Lefthand recognized Bisonhorn.

Whispers rustled around the circle, flitting from wolf to pony to boar, "They're coming! He says they're coming!"

Yes, Lefthand remembered, the reindeer were coming. He had seen them himself from the cliff top. High time the booming drum should hush.

Now, as smoke rises from a suddenly extinguished fire, a thin sound of talk and bustle drifted into the drum silence. The magic circle of beasts wavered, the line broke. The two ponies, gray and black, walked across the center together. The wolf head was shrugged off and the young man who wore it stood wiping sweat from his own face. On the far side of the broken circle the bison sagged. His rear end rose in the air and a man fought his way out from under it, while another man slithered out from the chest. The head dangled, horns sweeping snow.

Horrified, Lefthand watched. He had known what the magic beasts were — he had longed to be one himself. But to see magic dropped, cast aside in public, hurt his soul. There must be more ceremony than this.

He whispered to Snowbird, "Is that all?"

She turned an excited face to him. Her eyes shone with anticipation of adventure, of success and good food, but as she looked at him the joy faded from her face.

"No," Snowbird said, "that's not all. They break up this circle to form another, but that one will be secret." She looked at him intently and he was reminded of that horrible soft look of Bright's. Then she said, "Come to my fire, Lefthand. I have a little meat."

She did not wait for him to hump himself up. She sprang to her feet and walked quickly away into the swirl of the dispersing crowd. Jay let go of Lefthand and dodged after her. "I have a little meat," he had heard her say. Lefthand smiled wryly to himself as he struggled up alone and began the long, painful journey in the direction Snowbird had taken.

Men were hurrying around him, each to his own fire. Slinging his mask over his shoulder, each hunter grabbed the last shreds of meat from the embers and stood chewing, facing the river. The women silently raked the ashes with leg bones, hunting any tiny pieces of meat that might have flaked off the last roast. Any they found they handed up to the chewing hunters. All the faces shone with hope.

Snowbird's fire was the last, the farthest out toward the river. Three figures stood about it. The slim, dark one was Snowbird. She was raking the ashes, solemn as an old woman. She found two shreds of meat. She snatched them up hot in her hand and gave one secretly to Jay, holding it down behind her back. Jay was not in the least shy of her. He skipped up close to seize the tidbit but glanced warily at the third figure.

Lefthand paused. His heart turned cold. The third figure at Snowbird's fire was the Bear. He alone of the dancers had not discarded his magic. He stood, regally mysterious, his antlers branching into the fading sky, his pony tail curled about his feet. Only the bear paw had been pulled back from his wrist so that he could eat. The hand that emerged from the paw was thin, knotted, and mottled — the hand of an old man, the sorcerer. It was the only human item of his appearance, and Lefthand was not reassured. He felt the stab of the glance the sorcerer gave him from under the reindeer forehead. Nothing was said. The Bear stood quietly, eating and watching. Lefthand was sure the sorcerer saw into his own heart and knew the dismay he felt. He hesitated.

"Come to my fire," Snowbird had said. He had a right to be there.

And whom, after all, had he expected to see there? He knew that the sorcerer was Snowbird's father, as well as Bright's. Snowbird turned and saw him. Her look of invitation was stern and urgent. Lefthand understood. They saw that he was physically crippled. Now they waited to see if he were crippled inside, in the spirit. He gritted his teeth and set himself in motion. He lurched up to the fire.

Snowbird bent again over her embers and raked with the leg bone. She turned up a charred bit of meat. Looking at the sorcerer, she handed the bit to Lefthand. He found his hand holding it almost against his will. At the other fires only the hunters ate. He faced the Bear and waited.

Slowly the Bear nodded and for the first time Lefthand heard him speak. The voice was thin and cracked, an old man's voice to match the old man's hand that held the meat. It was a surprising voice to issue from that fearsome figure.

It said, "I will find you something to do in the hunt," and added a cackle that sounded incredibly like "tee-hee."

2

Darkness was rising from the land, flooding up the cliffs, when the hunters met on the riverbank. Behind them a crowd of fires glowed red among black tents. Shadowy women stood quietly about them. Strangely silent, the children ventured closer to the men, peering up curiously into the masked, almost unrecognizable faces of fathers and brothers.

Like the other hunters, Onedeer stood erect and remote. He was trying to concentrate his powers, to grow bigger inside. This was a night of magic. Tonight all these men would be transformed. A spirit would take possession of them and fill them with strength and speed greater than their own. Onedeer solemnly tried to forget himself and empty his mind to make room for the spirit, but he did not feel that he was succeeding. He felt unreal, alone, and somewhat sick in the stomach. His mask was heavy and damp with sweat, a dab of paint was melting down his nose and he hoped the men around him did not feel as he did. If they were all pretending, the magic would be powerless.

Swaying slightly, he brushed against his father, Bisonhorn. By the unresponding touch of Bisonhorn's arm, Onedeer knew that at least he was not pretending. The spirit was already strong within him. Bisonhorn was ready to work the magic upon the reindeer which would deafen their sensitive ears, smother their nostrils, and weigh down their tireless feet. Tonight Bisonhorn must not be himself, but something bigger and far more powerful. His eyes, resting on Onedeer, were glazed and unseeing.

For Onedeer, the magic was not complete. He could see Bisonhorn clearly, and the hunters beyond him, and the crowd of children pressing as close as they dared. One small face was looking up at him open-mouthed, the dark eyes wide with joyful surprise. Jay jostled against Onedeer and he backed off in a hurry, frightened by his contact with magic.

"Jay didn't think he would see *me* here!" Onedeer

chortled to himself. Then he wiped the thought from his mind. "I am not Me," he remembered sternly, "I am not Onedeer now, *I am the Hunter!*"

Between the children and the dark mass of tents two figures leaned together. Onedeer glanced at them and was again jarred to full consciousness. The girl-figure was his mother's young sister, Snowbird. The crooked shadow was Lefthand.

Onedeer looked at Lefthand as though from a great distance. Lefthand should be here with him now, stiff and sweating in a hard-won mask while waiting for the sorcerer. They had always been together. Together they had stalked hares, chipped spearheads, played at hunting, truly hunted. Then in a moonlit instant, Lefthand had been snatched away. He might as well be dead, now. That twisted figure leaning on a girl's strength could not be Lefthand.

Onedeer felt cold and empty, as though he was not even his full self without his friend. And in his loneliness the spirit found a foothold.

Now the silent children parted ranks and drew back. The last magician had come to the river. Slow and solemn, the Bear shambled between the rows of children who knocked each other over in hasty retreat. He swung his head as a bear does, glowering left and

right, but not at the children. His gaze was turned
inward, and he scowled at some image in his mind or
in the air. He swept by within arm's reach of Onedeer,
who almost stepped back but caught himself in time
and stood quietly.

Alone the Bear waddled ceremoniously down the
bank and out onto the ice. He was almost lost in the
thickening darkness before the hunters followed.
There was an aura about the sorcerer — a scent —
that kept people away from him. The spirit held him,
he was real. He was what they were pretending and
trying to be. When a safe expanse of ice stretched
behind him they followed, stepping gravely down the
bank and onto the ice. Dignity is essential to magic
and it would not do to slip.

They crossed the river at a slow, steady pace and
darkness was complete as they climbed the far bank.
Like a deer in a herd, Onedeer walked among the
men, following the vague shape of the man ahead and
feeling the pressure of the crowd around and in back.
He moved thoughtlessly, not knowing where he went,
and his head swam under the weight of the antlered
mask.

Now they were going downhill. The slope was steep
and there were obstacles. Here and there someone

carried a torch and by the reflections flashing on either side, Onedeer judged they were passing between rock walls.

They went single file here, steadily down, and the air that seeped under Onedeer's mask was stale. The combination of mask, darkness, and stagnant air was telling on Onedeer. He was no longer pretending or acting a part. He was truly no longer sure where he was, or even *who* he was. He knew with certainty only that he was part of a magical ceremony, and that the purpose of the magic was meat; meat, food, life.

Shuffling downward, gasping and clutching at the man in front of him, Onedeer remembered what his father Bisonhorn had told him. "Keep a picture in your mind. Try to see, for instance, a fat reindeer." He tried to see it.

The picture came with startling suddenness before his dark-baffled eyes. A reindeer stood facing him. It waggled its large, hairy ears and then it turned broadside to him, inviting a spear-thrust in its rounded side. It was a plump young doe with small, thrusting antlers. It would provide the tenderest meat Bright ever roasted.

Painted on the darkness, Onedeer saw the doe's hide shine like moonlight. He saw her eyes, wide and luminous, and beautifully stupid. In his mind he threw a spear and did not know that he had actually moved.

Light flared around him, red and sudden. Blinking, he saw the reindeer truly there. She was thinner than he had imagined her, and she was not standing still. She was running across his path, neck and four legs reaching, stiff and strange. He blinked again and she was still there, exactly the same. Then he knew that she was magic.

Light assailed Onedeer's eyes and now noise startled him. A drum was beating, thudding a staccato rhythm off the stone walls. The echo bounced around and up and down. Onedeer looked up as best he could in his flapping mask, and saw, stretched above him, the first roof of his experience.

Magic animals swept stretching horns across it, huge red bison, with tiny black hoofs rumbled overhead. The rock walls were alive with creatures who moved as the torchlight moved, and danced before the dancing hunters; a herd of bucks with spears rammed into their shoulders, red-spotted ponies, and a tusked boar.

Onedeer hardly knew that he was dancing. He shook his spear at the ponies. He stamped determination, he leaped hope. Then he jabbed and thrust with his antlers — a newfound motion — and jumped and

[83]

skipped like a fawn. He was the deer he sought, then he was the following hunter. Suddenly he knew he could not fail. Strength surged through his body, tingling in his veins. It was the strength of a hunter, the strength of meat in men's stomachs. Onedeer was lifted on a rising tide of faith, and hope, and determination.

From the center of the leaping, howling circle, the sorcerer watched. He alone stood still among the hunters, who, pounding and stamping, forgot their humanity and their limitations. Within the ponderous bearskin the tough old man smiled to himself. The hand that beat the drum ached, and he shifted to the other hand. His ankles shook, his knees wavered, but these weaknesses were hidden under the bearskin.

His power flowed like a strong stream through the secret chamber, and the hunters drank from it. He knew how to summon vast energies out of darkness, sudden light, and rhythm. And the magic animals who danced with the hunters were all his children.

3

Lefthand took the bone rake and stirred the embers of Snowbird's fire. The occasional charred scraps he turned up were bits of hare, and he wondered about them as he chewed. Snowbird came to sit beside him in the small circle of warmth. The night air was cold as death. Snowbird had paused to throw a hide over Jay, who was curled tightly in shivering sleep. As he uncurled a little she gave him a pleased, satisfied look.

"This is hare," Lefthand said, tasting judiciously. "How do you get it? Does your father hunt?"

She shook her head. "I trap."

"You what?"

"Trap. Look, like this." She reached over and grasped his coat. The skin was so blood-stiff and rotten that she easily ripped off a long strip. She laughed at his anger.

"I told you I would make you a new one. I take a piece of old skin like this and I tie it around a sapling where hares have been gnawing the bark. I leave the end like this . . ." She trailed the strip on the ground between them in a curious, repeating pattern. "Then I go off and think about something else."

"Along comes a hare looking for bark. He hops up to my sapling" — she hopped her hand up to the strip — "and maybe he puts a foot in my loop." One finger plopped into the waiting coil. "Then he thinks he will go away." She jerked up her finger and the strip tightened sharply about it. She jerked again, and the strip held fast.

Lefthand sat staring, thoughts rushing in his brain so hard he could feel them. At last he said, "Bright doesn't know how to do that."

"Oh yes, Bright knows. But you have to stay in one place a long time. You don't catch the hare the first day. And you people are always moving."

He thought that over for a time, while Snowbird wound the strip idly through her fingers, creating intricate and changing patterns.

"Why do you stay in one place?" he asked.

Without hesitation she explained. "Sorcerer is old. And he was never strong."

Lefthand looked at her, amazed. Who else would dare admit such a thing?

She went on: "In midwinter, when the new sun is born, the reindeer come down this valley. Then the people come, like now, and we have a big hunt. Sorcerer gets a good share of meat. I smoke it, and most times we have enough to last till spring. Then we

[86]

can fish in the river. And in summer there are plants to eat, if you know which ones are good."

Lefthand marveled at all this. He had never imagined such a life as she described — living in one place, watching the runs of hares, eating plants like a food animal. One thing especially he did not understand.

"Why does Sorcerer get a good share of meat?"

"Because he gives the hunters their strength."

"But how does he do that, if he has never been strong?"

Snowbird looked down. She looped the string back to the ground and let it lie. "I don't know what they're doing now. I don't know what it is. And then all winter he makes magic across the river . . . by himself. I don't know how."

A silence fell between them. He finally asked another question.

"Then you are alone all winter?"

She looked up at him. "I like having you here," she said with sudden warmth. "I hope you will stay. I think you had better stay."

Yes, Lefthand thought, if the old sorcerer would let him, this would be the life for a cripple.

A shadow approached out of darkness. Snowbird gasped and jumped up. Following her excited gaze, Lefthand saw three slow, bent forms coming toward them, two massive women supporting a third. The third woman stumbled passively along, letting herself be guided over the crumpled hillocks of snow and earth. Her eyes were bent on the burden she carried, clasped in her folded arms. As the trio slowly passed the smoldering campfires, women rose, girls leaped up, and they all followed. One fire after another was left to sputter to itself as the women gathered into a crowd which flowed silently through the darkness after the three bent figures.

Snowbird said not a word to Lefthand. Gathering her cloak about her she darted away after the others. He glimpsed her silhouetted against a farther fire and then he was alone with the embers and the sleeping Jay.

He sat, puzzled. Then he was aware of his heart beating, a small insistent thunder in his body.

Then he recognized it as a drum sound. Over there beyond the deserted fires a drum was tapped softly, so softly the reindeer herd upriver could not catch the sound. A fawn might notice a tingling in his blood, an unease, but it would not be sound.

A drum meant mystery. This mystery was wide and deep like a summer river. He felt it in the slow, tender rhythm.

[88]

Lefthand laid both hands flat on the ground and pushed himself to his knees. He gritted his teeth and raised one knee. By pushing on that knee with both hands, he got himself up, standing in his new, humped posture. He pressed his hurts with both hands and set off toward the drumming with the speed of curiosity.

The crowd had come to stand in a circle around a campfire. Here lay the third woman, the burdened one, on a soft skin nest. Her passive, wrinkled face bent down constantly, as did the eyes of the crowd, to the hare-skin bundle beside her.

The soft, gray hare skin wrapped a lazily moving form. A very small fist thrust up suddenly out of the skin. The mother caught the little waving hand gently in her hard, rough hand and folded it back into the skin. The crowd sighed.

The drum missed two beats and took up the rhythm again. Snowbird held it now, and tapped it with the tips of her fingers. She stood a little way back and the women gathered closer and took each other's hands. Snowbird's watching eyes were sad.

The dance was slow and gentle, with none of the leaping and stamping of the hunters' dance. It consisted of a slow shuffle sideways around the fire, the mother, and the squirming bundle. All the faces were quiet, all the eyes looked downward at the tiny bundle and inward to a communal understanding.

Lefthand saw Bright across the fire. The light caught on her rugged face a moment, the fall of her worn cloak, and her hand grasping a young, smooth hand. In another instant she passed into shadow and the girl beside her stepped sideways into the light. She was young, not much older than Snowbird. Though her body was thickening into mature lines, her face was still smooth and blank. Red hair tangled down her shoulders like an echo of the fire.

Snowbird tapped her drum and watched. A few girls younger than she stood about, and a few little boys. Lefthand looked in her face and saw there a longing, like his own.

He hobbled over to her and held out his hands. Snowbird started, seeing a male figure approach. Then she remembered, "only Lefthand." She smiled and handed him the drum.

Lefthand hardly missed a beat. He stood almost proudly, creating the dance, watching Snowbird slip happily into the ring. Bright and Red unlinked their hands and let her in between them. She moved, a lean, lithe figure silhouetted against the fire between two dumpy shapes. The circle moved tenderly about its incredible axis and Lefthand thought of Bright's baby with horror while he beat his little drum and watched. Some great mystery was here celebrated quietly, so quietly that the children, sleeping in warm little heaps like puppies, were not awakened. A great secret was being shared and he knew instinctively that the drum must stop, the dance break up, at the first suspicion of the hunters' return. He wondered that they allowed his own presence. Then he remembered. He, Lefthand, was not a man.

The cold bright stars were dimming when the drum stopped. The dancers continued their shuffling pace a moment longer, still hearing the drumbeat in their hearts. Then their ears recognized the silence. They stopped and dropped hands. A conscious, tired look came into their eyes; their faces drooped.

A crunch of snow and mumble of voices came out of the night and the circle broke hastily. Bright and Red ran to help the mother off her ceremonial nest and into the privacy of her tippy tent. The other dancers moved away, talking in loudly careless voices.

Lefthand set down the small pigskin drum and stepped in front of it. Two shapes were coming toward him from the direction of the river. He saw a pair of giant antlers move against the stars and then a smaller pair. He knew who the intruders were before they reached him.

Onedeer trotted up to Lefthand, with Sorcerer shambling a few steps behind. Onedeer held out his arms. Draped over his arms lay a beautiful fur, white as the moon, thick and soft as new snow. The bushy tail dangled to Onedeer's feet, the head lolled over his elbow.

"This," said Onedeer, holding it out to Lefthand, "is your part in the hunt. Put it on and come quickly."

Lefthand looked at the empty holes in the head that had once held yellow eyes of quick intelligence. He looked at the gaping mouth, still needled with teeth.

Sorcerer hobbled up to explain. "This time the scouts say there are no wolves. We will need a pretend one to turn the herd. You will do better than a real one. You will know what we want."

Lefthand took the fur. With a stiff movement he jerked it over his shoulders. The head fell on top of his own head and he felt himself already magically transformed. A wolfish strength surged through his torn, aching body. He felt able to do whatever it was Sorcerer wanted. Painful it might be, but his wolf-spirit would win over the pain — at least for the time of the hunt. His eyes met Onedeer's and he saw respect in Onedeer's look.

4

With the rising of the dawn wind the old doe opened cunning eyes. Most of the night she had lain dozing with shut eyes and open ears, head raised into the air current. Her nose never slept. Faint vibrations reached her half-conscious ears. They twitched sleepily, the doe dreamed of running, but the vibrations were too faint and far away to arouse her.

Wood smoke troubled the doe. Often it had been a premonition of violent disaster. Now the smell was so constantly in the air that her nose had almost ceased to record it. The valley air was permeated with it, there was no escaping it.

To the old doe, and to any of the reindeer sleeping around her, there was no other southward route. South they must go, toward the new sun, and this was the trail. This path had been worn by the pads of thousands of ancestors; it was known to their blood. There could not be another way.

Now the wind rose and shifted, blowing from the north. The pall of wood smoke was swept away down the valley, and with it all other beckoning or warning signals. But the doe still dreamed. The nightly smells had not been alarming.

As the first gray light spread along the eastern mountaintops, the old doe gathered her feet and pushed herself up. She shook snow from her rough coat and looked back at the others.

Behind her the resting herd snorted and grumbled. One by one the reindeer stood up, shook themselves, looked around for one more mouthful of moss before setting out. There was no moss to be had. The area had been scoured by their seeking hoofs the day before.

They would have to move on. They disliked moving with the wind. The herd coiled and wove about itself, hesitating. Coughing and blowing, the deer circled and pushed. Antlers clicked, clouds of snow puffed up from the milling feet.

Then the old doe started forward. Her pads pressed the snow determinedly and behind her the herd moved forward, at first by fits and starts, then faster and smoother until the snow was beaten solid under their steady passing. Uneasiness fell away as they walked. Only the foremost could smell anything but deer. The wind no longer mattered.

The old doe kept her eyes alert, her gaze darting from side to side. Her nose was useless now. To the east she watched the river, the ice-road. To the west she inspected the cliffs. A movement startled her.

She stopped. Between two boulders something had moved. The foremost deer drifted past her, watching too. The herd slowed almost to a standstill.

Whiteness slithered between the rocks. Behind a near boulder a face poked up. The doe saw it clearly in the strengthening light — white face, black nose, sharp ears. It was only a wolf. The doe was used to wolves. They followed the herd and sometimes pulled down a sick straggler. She paid them little attention unless she had a young fawn at her side.

She had not smelled this wolf on the fresh dawn wind and he was closer than a skulking wolf would usually come.

As she stood looking at him she caught a whiff of wood smoke, a herald of danger that was quickly blown away south.

The doe snorted and stamped a warning foot at the

wolf. Then she turned away, swinging toward the river. Behind her the herd swerved from the cliff and followed.

The wolf face lifted clear of the boulder and tipped its toothy grin to the sky. Lefthand very cautiously raised himself to watch the herd click past. Deer after deer came to the point where the doe had stopped, looked at him, and turned off toward the river. There were bucks with tremendous reaching antlers and does with smaller lighter weapons. Youngsters ran and jumped like heedless children among their sober elders. In his mind Lefthand stripped off all the gray and white hides and scraped and sewed them. He saw meat — neck and loin, haunch and shoulder — he saw antlers and bones that could be chipped into a thousand tools.

Lefthand knew that most of the reindeer walking by him would escape. The kill was limited by the number of hunters hiding under the riverbank, and by their strength. Even so, a happy greed swelled his heart. Success was almost assured. He had turned the herd as surely as any real wolf could have done it. Hunters made use of the wolves who stalked a herd. They would wait till the deer were startled away from the wolves and closer to the hunters. Sometimes wolves would enter into a deliberate partnership with the hunters, driving the deer within spear range. They had learned that the hunters would leave a fair share of guts for their wary helpers.

This time Lefthand was the helper and he could claim a share of guts for his work. It was a very humble part he played — Onedeer would never have accepted it — but Lefthand was eager to seize any chance at all to take part. He laughed gleefully, silently, as he watched the meat and hides drift past him toward the ambush.

Half of the hunting party were crouching under the riverbank, waiting for the herd to march within range. The other half waited farther down the valley in the shadow of the cliff. Attacked at the river, the reindeer would bolt toward the cliff where there would be a second attack. It was unlikely that any deer would turn back. Their minds were bent on going *forward*. If any did, the wolf could struggle out from the rocks to change their course.

Lefthand stifled an excited chuckle. A young buck paused to look at him, jumped nervously, and swerved away at a rapid trot. After him the remaining herd went by faster, raising clouds of snow which obscured the flashing gray bodies.

Hunks of snow slid down the cliff behind Lefthand and he jerked his head around. A reddish shape darted down beside him. It raised a fanged head and laughed at him. It was Snowbird in the coat of a summer-furred wolf.

He stared. For a moment he felt cheated of his role. But after all, why should she not join him? He was playing no part hallowed by tradition. Anyone could do this who was not qualified to do something better. And it was good to be able to share his glee. He grinned at Snowbird, accepting her presence, and the two mock wolves turned back to the herd.

The reindeer were thinning out now. Only a few stragglers trotted by: old reindeer, hobbling along, white ruffs bouncing on scrawny necks, one sick deer, hanging his head and stumbling; and an orphan fawn. He came trotting prettily, head erect on slender neck, delicate legs twinkling in the first ray of sunshine. Lefthand knew him immediately and positively. This was the fawn he had sketched in the snow, the fawn of the moonlit gorge. In his fever he had run in this fawn's body.

A shaft of doubt pierced his joy. What if this fawn, whose soul he had shared, should be killed? Should that moonlit flight, that night of fear and hope and maturing, lead only to death? Should the fawn, with all his feelings and perceptions, go into oblivion? The fawn would live on in the people who ate his tender meat, in the children who sucked his marrow and leaped and ran with his own energy. But he would not know it. For the fawn would be dead and with his own eyes he would never see moonlight or sunlight again.

For only a moment this realization chilled Lefthand. Then Snowbird nudged him and he came back to his own world.

She was pointing up the valley. The wonderfully docile old doe had led the herd very near the bank. Any minute now spears would fly, but the back half of the herd was wavering, turning back too soon to the cliffs.

Snowbird leaped out from behind the rocks. She ran, bent double, flapping and bouncing, toward the nearest straying deer. Lefthand squirmed out of the rocks and followed more slowly, holding onto his sore belly. The wolf head flopped up and down over his eyes so that he could scarcely see where he went. He came up against a rock and stopped, panting. Pushing back the mask he peered out across the valley.

The snow stretched wide and white to the ice and beyond to the brown-pitted cliffs. By the river the herd was now a broken gray line, spiky with antlers. The closer stragglers kicked up fluffs of snow. Farther along the cliff the wandering deer paused and watched the red wolf who was bounding up and down and howling in a thin, uncertain voice. They twitched their ears with wondering contempt.

Lefthand drew a deep and hurtful breath and raised his head. He intended to repeat and reinforce Snowbird's howls but he held his breath instead.

Across the rock, an arm's reach away, a face looked at him. Over the wrinkled white brow two pointed ears cocked toward Lefthand. Under a sharp black nose a long red tongue lolled, casual and easy. The wolf gulped, opened his mouth again, and blew strong breath in Lefthand's face.

Lefthand lay perfectly still against the rock. His heart froze and seemed to stop. He had no weapon with him. These wolves, though small, were strong, and he remembered fireside tales of their attacks on men.

Looking into the yellow eyes, he saw that he would need no weapon. The wolf was neither hungry nor afraid, neither stalking Lefthand nor startled by him. He had come to join him for a different reason.

The eyes spoke interest, partnership. "We are alike, you and I," was their message. "We are two predators together." Over the rim of rock the wolf's tail tip waved slowly back and forth, a plume of brightness in the morning sun.

Lefthand relaxed. Other tales came to mind now,

flitting ghostlike at the back of his consciousness. More often than not, the tales attested, approaching wolves were friendly.

The wolf's gaze shifted. He turned a pointed profile toward the river, ears attentively cocked. A moment later Lefthand also heard the noise — a distant, frantic roar. He dared to look away from the wolf toward the river.

The fuzzy gray line of deer had broken into a series of dots. Clusters exploded over the valley floor. Individual animals staggered alone, then collapsed. On the bank the men appeared as running, hurling blobs.

Lefthand forgot his weakness and pain, forgot even the suddenly vanished wolf. He set off at a limping, dragging run toward the red wolf. She was jumping and waving her arms and yelling at the handful of stragglers who had stopped. Heads up, ears stiff, as one deer they had turned their white rumps on the hunters and gathered all their fading strength to gallop back over hard-packed snow. With snowy ruffs streaming and nostrils heaving, they threw themselves into a hard trot that erased distance.

They were coming at an angle to bypass the shouting wolves. Lefthand flung himself out before them. He waved his arms and howled. In a moment the racing deer were all around him. They flashed by, terror-glazed eyes watching him sideways. He saw the foam on their lips and smelled their bodies as they rushed past, while he had to stand weaponless.

He hung his head and let the last few deer dash by without attempting to stop them. He saw only their hoofs thundering on the hard snow. Then four slender legs pumped past, little black hoofs winking sunshine. With head down and forward, shoulders hunched, the fawn presented only a fast vanishing white rump, propelled by strong swinging hind-quarters. Lefthand stood watching while the white-ness of the fawn vanished against the snow. For a time the dark legs could be seen dwindling, and sometimes the smudge of his head and ears, until the vast, white morning took him.

5

"Walk," a voice twittered in Lefthand's ear, "keep walking. If you lie down you'll never get up." Left-hand was stooping to crawl into Provider's tent when Sorcerer grabbed him from behind. Bony fingers clawed his shoulders and Sorcerer pushed him away from the tent, back into the crowd.

The one thing Lefthand really ached to do was to creep into a tent, pull a robe over his head, and shut out the world. Sorcerer had taken away the white wolf skin, and with it his magic strength. Now he was again a cripple, wandering painfully about the camp, avoided by everyone. With Sorcerer spying on him there was no help for it; he could do nothing but limp around, feel his pain and look and listen.

After the tremendous slaughter on the riverbank the camp had been moved. This was no great trouble. The women simply collapsed their tents, rolled up their few goods on the baggage sleds, and moved out to camp among the corpses. Now the tents sprawled among pegged skins and piles of innards. Meat strips dangled to darken over small fires. All over camp the women worked merrily, spicing labor with talk. A steady drone rose into the air, a constant hum of happy voices interrupted by laughter. One of these voices, momentarily raised in argument, was familiar. Lefthand turned hopefully toward it.

"I know, I know, your son is a handsome boy," it said loudly, "but I want more than that! I don't care if he is handsome. I'm looking for a *man*. Onedeer is too young."

"What are you, Red, an old woman?" The answering, chuckling voice was Bright's.

Bright, Red, and Snowbird were kneeling on a bloody skin. Eight sharp bone pegs held the skin taut while they worked rhythmically together. First Red would throw herself forward, dig her scraper into the middle of the skin, and pull it back to herself. As she withdrew, leaning back on her heels, Bright would dive in from the other side; and as she leaned away, Snowbird would come in between them. Working at this happy, swinging pace, they would have that skin clear of blood and clinging fat before the sun reached its height. Lefthand knew what Snowbird planned to do with it. It was the skin of an old, barren doe, the first reindeer killed from the ambush, and Bright had given it to Snowbird for a special purpose.

Lefthand moved slowly toward the familiar group. He wanted to hear Bright's comforting voice and he wanted to see how his doe skin was progressing. As he crept forward he crossed the path of three young men who were striding together, boasting loudly with large gestures. They stopped abruptly at sight of Lefthand. He stood still for them but they hesitated to pass in front of such an evil apparition.

They were red-faced, big-shouldered young men, full of meat and laughter. Two were dark and ruddy.

The middle one was blond and blue-eyed and the shadow of grief crossed his face as he looked at Lefthand. It was Onedeer. Then he laughed and pointed out to his friends a way around Lefthand. They passed behind him, three in step together, and walked away into the crowd, leaving him behind.

Lefthand saw Red look after Onedeer. She shot out a strong white arm to point at him and then swung around to point at a silent group of hunters crouching together, happily sucking marrow from a pile of bones.

"That one," he heard her say. "'Your man's brother."

"Provider?"

"Yes, Provider. That's what I'm looking for, a *hunter*. He didn't get that name sitting around all day sucking marrow!" With a teasing smile she added, "He's almost as handsome as Onedeer!"

Snowbird remarked softly, "I'd want one younger."

Red explained in her carrying voice, "You don't know how a young one will turn out! He might be no good. He might even turn out like that poor beast who can't even stand up straight!"

"You mean Provider's son," Snowbird told her, angrily.

"Provider's son!" Red stopped work. She leaned on

her scraper in the middle of the skin, staring open-mouthed at Snowbird. Obvious thoughts galloped through her mind.

Bright cast a look like a spear at her sister. A new hope had been dawning in her starved heart. In a few days she would have to pack her sled and go trudging off into the endless world with her silent men. Perhaps this big, hearty girl who liked to talk could be persuaded to come.

She began to talk. In her haste she stumbled over words and forgot them and said them again. Words came tumbling and flopping like young birds from a nest, as Bright explained to Red what had happened. Lefthand was not born like that, she assured her. "It happened a moon ago, and in any case he won't be coming with us," Bright said, just as Lefthand's shadow fell across the skin.

Bright's voice trailed away and the two girls looked up. They grinned at Lefthand and Red bent to her scraping again. She scraped briskly, Snowbird thoughtfully. Bright was flustered and she missed two turns.

"Come on, Bright," Red scolded, "you're missing!" Bright went back into action and Red returned to the subject on her mind, just as though there were no boy within hearing distance.

"He *is* a fine, handsome man," she said, "and a

good hunter. You don't often go to sleep hungry, do you?"

"Not often," Bright hastily agreed, and added slyly, "He's lonely."

Lefthand slumped, looking down at the three heads, black and red and gold-gray, which swooped by turn across the skin. The blades bit, the words flew. They were women's words, small and gossipy. After a while he turned and wandered away to watch other groups, listen in on other conversations.

A rushing gang of children almost swept him off his feet. Behind the gang ran Jay, a string of intestines flying from his fist.

Near Lefthand the gang stopped in a huddle, with Jay hopping up and down on the outside. Lefthand watched him sadly. No one, not even the children, wanted to have much to do with a boy whose brother had been mauled by a bear.

The gang jiggled and squirmed with excitement as one little boy broke from its center and dodged inside the nearest tent. He came out smiling smugly, with something white clasped in his sooty little arms. He disappeared in the shouting, jumping mass of children. Lefthand drew nearer and lowered himself gently onto the packed snow well away from the gang but close enough to see the game.

The huddle broke up and from it came a procession of little girls. They pranced and minced in single file, fingers spread from their foreheads like antlers. The little boys threw themselves prone on the snow and wiggled, bottoms up, skillfully stalking. Lefthand nodded to himself, pleased at their craft. He and Onedeer had wiggled just so through many a serious game.

Then, like sickness, a cold sorrow spread through his vitals. He saw the little boy wrap himself in mysterious whiteness. It was the wolf skin in which he, Lefthand, had turned the herd. The head bobbed on the little boy's chest and the tail thumped after his heels. He lolloped along, leaping and squatting with a staccato motion — exactly the motion of a cripple pretending to be a wolf.

From what vantage point had this sharp-eyed child been watching? Lefthand grimaced and bit his tongue. At the same moment shouting erupted from the bubbling stream of adult voices.

Into the mock hunt burst a huge, lumbering woman, red-faced with fury, swinging a powerful open hand. She knocked the proud little lead doe off her feet. She charged down the line of tripping reindeer, sending the slow ones sprawling, while the more alert shied away and trotted to a safe distance.

The little wolf saw her coming. He tried to run, but his path was blocked by the stalkers scrambling in all directions. Before he could move the roaring woman had caught him in a bear hug, ripped the wolf skin from his shoulders, and sent him staggering with a resounding box on the ear.

Lefthand sat grinning, delighted. He would gladly have broken up the hunt with equal violence. He watched with relish after the little boy who stumbled away crying, pressing his ear with his palm.

Meanwhile the woman hugged her wolf skin. She rocked it in her arms like a baby. Murmuring to it, she carried it back to her tent.

Behind her the children collected again, laughing. They brushed snow from knees and shoulders. Some of the little girls swung their arms, practicing for the day when they would be mothers. Then like a swarm of bees the gang seemed to rise in the air, barely skimming the snow as they flew away to play another game. Jay ran behind, earthbound, but flapping hopefully.

Lefthand was suddenly seized from behind and dragged to his feet.

"You've sat around long enough," growled the Bear. "You're going to stretch those muscles!" And he turned Lefthand about and propelled him back to the doeskin. Bright, Red, and Snowbird looked up amazed as Lefthand was pushed to his knees in their circle.

"Give him your scraper, Red," the sorcerer ordered. "This boy is going to get a workout, ha-ha!"

Slack-jawed, Red stared. Sorcerer snarled at her, swiped a paw at her, and she hastily tossed the scraper across the skin to Lefthand.

"Now," said Sorcerer, bending over him, "you know well enough what to do. Let's see you do it!" He stamped and snorted like a suspicious pony as Lefthand gingerly reached out his hand and set the scraper in the center of the skin.

"No, no, boy, two hands! And reach out with your belly!"

Lefthand stretched and groaned.

"That's it, that's it. Put the belly and the back into it and earn your new coat!" The sorcerer giggled, whirled about, and hare-hopped away.

Lefthand scowled stormily after him.

"You'd better do it," Bright advised.

"Sorcerer knows what's best," Snowbird encouraged.

Red snorted, got to her feet, and moved away. She had no scraper now and she did not think it wise to witness Lefthand's disgrace. She could not be sure the sorcerer would fail to cure him. This wreck might yet be walking around like a man.

Viciously, grunting with pain and anger, Lefthand bent to the scraping. "There!" he told the skin, and "There!", wishing it were the sorcerer's back. The skin ripped, a small red hole opening under his angry hand.

"Lefthand," Bright murmured, "not so rough. Work in the corner, where it won't matter."

A shrill yell ripped across the low hubbub around them. "Look at the cripple! He's *working!*"

With a swirling rush Jay's gang surrounded them. The little boy with the swollen red ear pointed at Lefthand and screamed derision. Other boys threw themselves on the snow, scraping and grunting. The little girls staggered and howled with laughter.

Lefthand straightened. He put his shoulders back, regardless of the hurt. He was holding Red's scraper like a spear and he stared coldly at the swollen-eared boy.

Laughter died. The children drew away, astonished and fascinated.

"Hey!" said the boy softly, and he stepped back.

Then Lefthand's fury-hazed vision cleared. The boy was not an enemy, only a jeering personification of the hostile camp. He was actually no larger than Jay.

Lefthand lowered the blade.

Instantly Snowbird jumped up and over the skin. She threw off the pretense of being grown up as she would throw off a cloak.

"I'll race you!" she called to the gang. "I'll race you to the drum!" And she was gone, swooping away among the fires, the children screeching at her heels. Only Jay hung back, looking at Lefthand with sorrowful wonder.

"Sorcerer's coming!" Bright warned, and Lefthand scraped with her, stretching and wondering that it hurt less. His arm reached easier and his shoulders tingled.

6

In the clear, chill evening the twins came to Bright's fire. They sat close to the coals, wriggling their toes and their noses, tasting in anticipation the haunch of reindeer she poked out of the ashes. Sparks popped up and spiraled lazily to join the stars. Other cooking fires flared around them. The rich smell of roasting meat overhung the valley. In good-natured silence the twins watched as Bright raked the haunch out onto the snow. Then they attacked it with blades and hands.

For some time the camp was almost silent, as men at all the fires tore and munched and gulped.

When the hands reached more slowly and beards shone greasy in the firelight, Bright said, "Provider."

Startled, both men looked at her. In their company she had long ago given up talking. When she did speak, she usually addressed only Bisonhorn.

"Provider, you know that girl, Red?"

Chewing loudly, he stared.

"The big girl with red hair."

He nodded.

"If you ask her, she will come with us."

Provider looked into the fire. After a silent while he got up and wandered away. He went vaguely, round-about, more or less in the direction of Red's fire.

FIVE

THE SORCERER

1

LIKE A SQUIRREL scrambling out of a dark tree hole, Sorcerer emerged from his magical disguise. He lifted off the gigantic, antlered mask and Lefthand was astonished to see his little, wrinkled face — the face of a very old man — laughing and jiggling with glee at meeting the sun.

He skipped out of the sacred skin and left it heaped on the snow. One by one he shook his bony arms and legs. His whole right side was shrunken and withered. The right arm was half the size of the left arm. Both were stretched joyfully to the shining sky.

Finally, Sorcerer put his tousled white head down and turned a somersault. Leaping up, he laughed at Lefthand's amazement. "You'll be doing that yourself before I'm done with you," he said. Lefthand did not want to imgaine himself doing any such thing. Provider had never, in his memory, turned a somersault.

Quietly impatient, the others waited. Spears in hand, they stood around Bright's dying fire, in the midst of other dying fires. The last of the crowd was now a faint, moving patch downriver, weaving along like a distant herd. The tent-town had vanished in its own smoke. The hundred smoldering coal piles and the thin layer of waste scattered over the area — scraps of bone, hide and offal — told of human habitation. The next storm would erase these signs.

Two small tents still huddled under the cliff — Sorcerer's and Lefthand's, a parting gift from Bright and Red. From the meat rack between the tents hung the stripped meat of three reindeer carcasses.

Provider indicated these with a scornful hand. "What are you going to eat?" he asked. "Those will not last long."

He stood closest with the women while Bisonhorn and Onedeer hovered well away, poised to go.

Sorcerer laughed. "Three deer for three people! When they are gone, I can still scuttle about some,

Provider! One does not have to eat bison hump or reindeer haunch — I could surprise you with the things I eat. Hare, piglet, rat — anything that comes along.

"Your boy. I will cure him. Come back when the new sun wanes and you will see him dance in a bear skin!"

Provider obviously did not believe it.

"Look how straight he stands now, with the exercise I give him! A young boy like that, you can do anything with him. No need to despair!"

Provider frowned with intense embarrassment. Lefthand had noticed before this how incautiously the sorcerer talked. Like a woman, he jabbered anything that crossed his mind, often acting out his words with gestures and dancing. Now he jumped up and down, pointing insistently to Lefthand.

"That boy will hunt. He will do more than that."

Sorcerer came close to Provider and thrust his white head forward to touch the younger man's chest. Provider stepped back.

"I will take your son across the river." A wizened finger pointed at the wide, white ice. "I have secrets over there — magic secrets. You told me yourself that your son has magic in his left hand." Sorcerer stepped back and laughed. "When you see him again, you will call him by another name!"

With a final, malicious titter at Provider, the old man turned to Bright. He folded her large form in his lean arms, rather as a spider embraces a fly. Provider and Lefthand looked long at one another. There was hope in Provider's eyes, seeming to say, Maybe the sorcerer can do it. Maybe I will see you here again. But they warned, I don't want to see you like this again.

Lefthand's eyes answered, I know it.

Bright turned and picked up the lead of her baggage sled. Red took her lead. Bisonhorn and Onedeer sprang away like eager bucks, sniffing new smells, searching the landscape.

They had forgotten Jay. Anguished, he hovered, stepping now after the departing women, now back to Lefthand. Deciding, he ran to Lefthand and caught his arm in a desperate, hurting grip. Lefthand shook him off but Snowbird reached out and pressed him against her.

The men were soon gray brown specks in the distance. The women followed more slowly, backs bent, heads together, talking as they went.

Lefthand knew how Red felt, stumping away into a

new life. He felt Bright's relief. No sick baby, no wounded boy burdened her. She swung along like a young woman.

The men's eyes were on the far distance. They watched continually for a brown speck to move, for a deer to stand up and shake snow from its flanks.

Lefthand bitterly watched them go, the company of the strong. It would take a tremendous magic to make him whole. He did not believe that this queer, woman-ish old man could do it.

2

"But Snowbird," Jay protested, "that's too big for me! See?" He flung himself down on his back on top of the skin. "It goes down to my feet. How can I run in it?"

Snowbird laughed. Kneeling hunched over the skin she sewed steadily. Her bone needle punched in and out, in and out, and drew the twisted sinew tight and firm through both edges of skin. Under her strong, quick hands a jacket was taking shape. She pushed Jay aside and went on working.

"It isn't for you," she said.

"Oh!" Jay was used to being thought of, taken care of, first. He had assumed that any new garment made from a fine skin must be for him. It took him the space of a breath to figure it out.

"It's for Lefthand!" Jay sat up abruptly.

"Yes."

Snowbird spoke softly, almost secretly, but Jay felt no embarrassment. "Lefthand!" He called shrilly, "Lefthand!" He hopped up and went off around the tent in search of his brother. Left alone, Snowbird bit off the sinew, tied a knot, and began sewing up the other side of the jacket.

On the far side of the tent a powerful odor hit Jay like a fist. It was the smell of Lefthand, a sickening stink of mixed blood and sweat. There he was, standing fifty steps away from a small fire. Balanced in its embers was a stone bowl reeking with the stench of blood. Sorcerer leaned above it, muttering and poking in it with a reindeer leg bone.

Sorcerer was an even more startling figure without his Bear costume than with it. His hair, thin and scraggly and pure white, tangled to his bony shoulders. Jay had never seen such white hair before. It spoke of unimaginable age. The face that looked up at Lefthand was wrinkled as the palm of a hand. Almost lost in the wrinkles, small blue eyes shone forth a startling intelligence. The grotesque body, one half gracefully agile, the other dead and shriveled gave a nightmarish impression. The sorcerer looked more spirit than human, more a magic being than a mortal one.

But Jay had huddled with him in his tent on several cold nights. He had gnawed bones Sorcerer tossed his way and found good meat on them. He moved close to the awesome figure and looked over his shoulder.

"Auk!" said Jay, "what's *that?*" In the stone bowl bubbled a gray, slow-writhing mass.

Sorcerer chuckled and mumbled something about magic. Then he said distinctly to Lefthand, "Take off your clothes."

Lefthand came stiffly forward to the fire. He moved much more easily now than when they first came to the valley and he stood almost straight, though his movements were jerky and brought a look of dumb pain to his brown eyes. With clumsy fingers he tried to untie the sinews that held the filthy jacket rigidly together.

Quickly Jay ran to help him. "I'll do it, Lefthand."

Sorcerer held up a commanding hand. "Lefthand

must do it himself. If he is helped by anyone else" — the blue eyes fixed Jay warningly — "*anyone* else, the magic will fail."

So Jay stood helpless, watching Lefthand's weak fingers pull and tug. It took a long time. A cloud spread across the sun as Jay and Sorcerer waited, but at last the sinews came apart.

"Take it off," Sorcerer ordered. Lefthand began gingerly working the jacket off his shoulders and down his arms, while Sorcerer turned back to the bowl with its bubbling mess. He flexed his hands, tipped his head back, and shut his eyes. Mumbling all the while, he reached out both hands, grabbed the bowl, and lifted it off the fire. He set it down in the snow where it hissed and steamed as if in protest. Then he licked his hands and pressed them flat on the snow.

Lefthand had managed to get the jacket off. He stood upright, nearly bare before the fire, with all his wounds, healed and half-healed, exposed to the sun. His face was impassive as rock.

Sorcerer smiled. His smile was as warm as Bright's. Like hers, it spoke of kindness. But unlike Bright, Sorcerer had knowledge. He not only wished to help Lefthand; he knew how.

"Let it cool." He pointed to the gray stuff, still slightly bubbling in the stone bowl.

"What is it?" Lefthand asked. He spoke through lips tight with dread, and the words came out harshly.

"It's only fat. You saw me put it in the bowl. It's just a lump of reindeer fat. Bear fat would be better but we don't have any." Lefthand looked uncertainly at the hot, liquid stuff. He had never seen fat in that condition before. Bright lugged no stone bowls in her baggage sled.

Sorcerer dipped a finger experimentally in the fat, snatched it out, and sucked it violently. "With this you will heal smooth," he said, speaking around the finger.

"Lefthand!" Snowbird's call seemed to come from a distance. Lefthand was looking at the fat and at the sorcerer standing firmly before him, determined to do something to him as soon as the fat cooled. He was sunk in fear and distrust. He heard Snowbird's voice, looked up, and saw her running toward him. She was holding something out to him.

"I finished it," she said, and came up beside him. She held something before his face.

It was his new jacket. It smelled only of smoke and deer. Lefthand had not worn a new garment, made especially for him, since he was small. His own mother had made his last new outfit. Bright had mended and altered it and then remade the men's old clothes to fit him, but any new, boy-sized garments she made were for Onedeer or for Jay.

He reached out and took the jacket with trembling hands.

"This is beautiful," he said to Snowbird, and watched her eyes light up with pleasure.

"I have some painted bones," she said, "to sew around the edges. I can put them on any time. Don't wear *that* again." With a scornful foot she kicked the old jacket aside.

"Snowbird," Sorcerer broke in, "go work on the leggings. There's a snowstorm coming and you will soon have other things to do."

"A storm?" Snowbird glanced at the bright sky.

Lefthand nodded. "Clouds are coming." Even as he said it, another cloud passed before the sun and the world was swept with gray shadow.

"I'll hurry your leggings," Snowbird said. "You'll have them tonight." She thrust the new jacket into Lefthand's arms and darted away.

"Now," said Sorcerer, and he dipped his hands in the warm fat. Lefthand handed the garment to Jay. "Hold it," he said, and stood very still, watching the sorcerer's greasy hands approach his scars.

"It won't be bad," Sorcerer murmured, "just a little warm." With firm, quick fingers he smeared the fat over the scars and livid bumps of Lefthand's wounds. "Breathe deep," he instructed. "Go limp where it hurts." Lefthand obeyed. He breathed as slowly as a sleeper, relaxing his screaming muscles. The hurt faded with the sunshine.

3

Toward evening snowflakes began to tumble out of a steadily dimming sky. Jay threw his head far back and stared up at them until they seemed to come pelting up at him from a deep, gray abyss. He tottered and staggered, almost afraid of falling into that cold depth. The snowflakes whirled, growing larger and darker as they circled up to strike him on the face and dive dryly into his mouth.

He heard a giggle nearby, swallowed a snowflake, and jerked up his head. The world swung back into place, sky above and earth beneath. Beside him Snowbird teetered, head back and mouth open, reeling to catch the flakes on her tongue.

Lefthand watched, relishing silent disapproval. Had she nothing better to do than to chase snowflakes?

Maybe there was a white hare struggling in one of the traps among the willows. Then another, louder giggle caught his ear.

With a sinking heart, Lefthand turned around and stood appalled.

Behind him the sorcerer swayed, arms outstretched, head flung back. He held his wide mouth open and the snowflakes swooped in. He did not have to chase them, so thickly was the snow coming.

Lefthand could not imagine his father or Bison-horn playing like children. These people had no dignity. Watching the foolishness, he felt cut off from his people and his life by more than distance.

He would be the adult in the group, he decided. He would go to the traps alone.

He set off, walking slowly out of habit rather than actual pain. His new outfit was soft and clean and pliant. Almost gracefully he was walking away when Sorcerer called after him, "Where are you going, Lefthand?"

Lefthand flung over his shoulder, "To the traps," and Snowbird gasped surprise. "Alone?"

"Why not?"

"Stop," said the sorcerer. Lefthand stopped. Sorcerer's foolish moments only made his authority more pressing when he chose to use it.

"There is no time for that," he said softly. Left-hand turned to look at him. So thick was the storm now that he could hardly see the others. They were merely gray blobs in a white whirl.

"The traps will wait," said Sorcerer. "Now we're moving."

"To the rock tent?" Snowbird asked.

"That's the place to be in a storm like this. You pack the meat and wood. I take the fire. The tents can sit here."

Snowbird ran toward the faint blur of the tents, Jay at her heels. Feeling Sorcerer's gaze upon him, Left-hand followed. This packing of sleds was not his work, but then, what was? He might as well be of some use. He came to Sorcerer's tent just as Snowbird wriggled out, three small frozen carcasses piled against her chest.

Carried like that, they reminded him of . . . of babies! Lefthand's world was suddenly dark. He seemed to see a monster rising out of the tent, carry-ing heaped death and sorrow. The hares' stiff, stretched legs were like thin babies' legs, the little mouths were seekingly open. A pitiless face grinned at him over the corpses. "You get the wood," Snowbird said.

[126]

Lefthand blinked the vision away. The world became itself again. It was not a monster he saw going past him to the sled, but a handsome, competent girl packing meat for her family.

These flashes of vision were usually so quickly over that Lefthand was barely aware of them. This one he would remember. Ducking into the tent he scolded himself. "That's what's wrong with me! Onedeer doesn't see things like that!"

Searching in the dark among stone bowls, strings of teeth, and bone tools, he found the scattered sticks and twigs. This work was definitely unworthy, but Lefthand obediently thrust the sticks out to Jay's waiting hands. He was almost accustomed to the sorcerer's ridiculous ways.

He squirmed out to find the others leaving, already vanishing. A white-speckled red haze moving ahead was Sorcerer's torch. Snowbird was pulling the laden sled, which suddenly became heavy as Jay ran and plunked his weight upon it.

"Oof!" she gasped, "Lefthand, help me!"

"He doesn't have to ride," Lefthand growled. But he did help, putting his mittened hand beside hers on the strap.

"Is it far, this rock tent?"

[127]

"The other side of the river. In the cliff."

"You can find it?" They were not keeping pace with the trotting torch.

"I've been there before."

They pulled then in silence, faces down, flying snow stinging their eyes. Down the bank they went with a rush and out on the ice, stepping where the new snow was fluffy. The torch was already far out on the river, all but lost in the storm. The sled swerved and shied behind them and Jay chuckled happily. Once Lefthand glanced back and saw him sitting upright with his mouth open and his eyes crinkled shut.

At the far bank they paused. Lefthand warned, "Jay, you have to get off."

"Mmm," said Jay.

Lefthand turned and grabbed the sled and tipped Jay off. Snowbird sighed, picking up the cargo, and Lefthand scrambled up the bank. He hauled up the sled and looked into blankness. The torch was gone.

"Where to?" he asked, as Snowbird and Jay packed the sled.

"I'll lead." Snowbird walked ahead, stooped into the storm. Lefthand caught Jay's little hand and pushed the strap into it. Together they pulled the sled along Snowbird's track.

"What's a rock tent?" Jay wondered aloud.

[128]

"A tent made of rock," Lefthand reasoned.

"Can it hold us all? How can it be made of rock?"

"Jay, I don't know! You just pull." They stumbled on, blinded by the rushing flakes and the gathering night.

"This is it," said Snowbird, and stopped.

They had come slam up under the mountain. Right before their feet lay a bare, sheltered strip of earth. Sorcerer squatted there, his torch flickering undisturbed. No snow fell.

Lefthand looked up at the stone wall behind Sorcerer. At the height of three men it leaned out. It kept leaning out and out, making a roof like a tent over the bare ground. Tilting his head back Lefthand saw that the cliff swept out far above their heads, and finally came to a jagged edge. Here the snowflakes hit and bounced, then drifted down to form the ridge of snow in which he was standing.

He stepped in under the cliff and out of the drift, jerking the sled after him. This, then, was the rock tent. Open to the air, it spread itself over one, shutting out the sky and the falling cold.

Lefthand sighed happily. He pushed back his hood and looked around. He could see the others almost clearly. Their bustling shapes were obscured only by darkness which Snowbird was busily dispelling. She crouched at the extreme back of the shelter, building a tiny tent of twigs. Sorcerer thrust his torch under the twigs, then leaned over Snowbird, rubbing his hands and whistling softly. As a little flame licked up, it threw his shadow on the rock wall.

"Oooo," cried Jay, pointing, "look at the pony!"

The flame sank down again before Lefthand could see where Jay was pointing.

"Aha!" tittered the old man. "Aha, yes, there are ponies here!"

Again the fragile light rose and wavered over the twig tent. A faint glow warmed the wall and a pony stood proudly behind Sorcerer's head.

By its stillness Lefthand saw immediately that it was magic. It stood as high as a real pony. Its head was up, mane bristled, tail streaming out in silent wind.

Without hesitation Lefthand walked over to it. He was drawn by it as though to the presence of something well known, cherished, and a little feared. The pony's long, hopefully fat body was made of red ocher rubbed on the rock. Its little black hoofs, lifting from the earth, were soot. Lefthand thought of all the magic animals he himself had made. He had drawn them in mud, in sand, in snow, where the first rain had wiped them away as though they had never been.

Why had he never thought to use paint? And on hard rock?

He examined the pony carefully, awed and excited. And the sorcerer watched him.

"That magic is dead," the old man said finally. "It was good once, but that was long ago. No pony has been seen in this valley since I was little, like Jay."

Jay uttered a croak of disbelief. His thoughts were plain in the wide eyes that stared at Sorcerer. Surely this withered being, with his thin white hair and his wide-spaced teeth, could never have been little like Jay!

"Oh yes," Sorcerer insisted, smiling at Jay. "We are all little at first. We do not all reach my age." And he glanced down at his body with profound satisfaction. "Not many of us reach my age, but we all start out little." The sharp old eyes strayed from Jay's face to Lefthand, who was still inspecting the painting, then to Snowbird, bent over encouraging her fire. "When I was little I slept many nights in this place. My mother had her fire where ours is tonight."

"Was this pony here then?" Lefthand wondered. He dared to touch the haunch, which was painted on a bunching mass of rock. It threw just the right shadow on the belly.

"The red pony, yes, he was here when we came. My father made the other one."

Sorcerer waved a hand to the left. Lefthand started, looking into the darkness. Just visible at the edge of the firelight were the eyes, nose, and ears of a black pony, facing the red one.

"You saw him do it?" Lefthand tore his eyes from the paintings and looked at Sorcerer with sudden hope. If Sorcerer knew how . . .

"Yes, I watched. He did not let the women or the children watch, only the hunters. I was so small I didn't matter or he didn't see me. Or maybe that's why the magic failed."

"The magic failed?"

"The ponies never came."

Lefthand could hardly believe it. The ponies were wonderfully real.

"Why?"

"Well," he grunted slowly, "maybe it was because I watched. Maybe it was because of this place. You see," Sorcerer gestured out toward the valley, "this is an open place. Anyone can see it. Too many eyes weaken a magic. And then, there's the wind. Snow never falls here, rain never falls here, but the wind blows by. Maybe the wind blew the magic away in the air." They looked, following his gesture, and saw the cold emptiness a step away, the snowflakes gleaming harshly as they drifted past the firelight. Sitting down, they drew as close as possible to the little fire that now murmured and crackled to itself under the hoofs of the red pony.

"The magic blew away," Lefthand prompted, "and what did you do?"

Sorcerer shivered. He trembled as though the cold outside had reached through his deerskin clothes and gripped his body. But Lefthand knew the coldness came from within.

"Then we were hungry. My mother knew how to trap hares, but there were none. Every day we went out together, she and I, to set the traps. And we could not see where to set them, because there were no tracks."

"What did you do?"

"We just tied the thongs anywhere, and hoped a hare would find one."

Snowbird shook her head. "It wouldn't."

"No. Every day my father and his two friends went hunting. Sometimes they caught a rat and that was how we lived."

Lefthand looked across the fire into the sorcerer's face. It was shadowed, haggard, the eyes looking inward to a terrible memory. Every twinkle of good humor was wiped off that face and Sorcerer continued to tremble.

"That was the first winter the ponies did not come. They never came again. That winter even the reindeer did not come.

"One day it dawned cold, snow falling so thick you could not see where you went — like now. You know, Lefthand, this is not the time to go hunting. You don't see the animals if they are there. You don't see their tracks because the snow swallows them up. Wouldn't you say this is a time to sit by the fire and chip spearheads?"

Lefthand nodded. He feared the look in Sorcerer's face — a dangerous spirit lurked behind the old man's eyes. But he wanted very much to know how the story ended. Sorcerer was here, after all. He had survived somehow to sit in the rock tent this night and remember. How had he done it? Or rather, how had his father done it?

"My father and his friends went hunting. They went down by the river looking for pigs. There had been no pigs there since the summer. There were no pigs that day.

"They came back to the cliff, looking for hare. If there were hares running in the snow, they did not see them. You know how tired you feel when you are very hungry?"

The three young heads all nodded promptly.

"They were ready to come back here and rest with us by the fire, when my father smelled . . ." Sorcerer paused, wrinkling his nose and looking around at his tense audience, ". . . wood smoke!"

" 'Ah,' said my father, 'There are people nearby! Maybe they have meat.' "

Sorcerer stopped telling. He looked into the fire and shivered, and Snowbird had to ask him gently but urgently. "And then?"

And Jay piped eagerly, "And then!"

"They followed the smoke trail and in a little while they came to the fire. Down there." He pointed vaguely south. "There was a man sitting alone by the fire. He looked up when he heard their voices and he was a man they did not know."

Abruptly, Sorcerer stopped shivering. He raised his head as though seeing approaching strangers and Left-hand knew that he was acting the story for them as his father had acted it for him on this spot.

"They had never seen him at the dances, you know. They had never seen anyone like him anywhere. He was small" — Sorcerer hunched down into himself to

[135]

show how small — "and his head hung down like this." He jabbed his chin into his chest. "His shoulders were bigger than all the rest of him." Sorcerer bunched his shoulders and shrugged violently.

"He looked at them like this" — Sorcerer's face took on a heavy, stupid look — "and he said 'uggarmgg.'" Jay laughed nervously, but no answering mirth flickered in Sorcerer's remembering eyes.

"He was hairy, hairy all over, like a bear. They only knew he was a man because of the fire. Well, my father stepped up and asked him, did he have any meat? They knew he had. They could smell it roasting and the smell drove them mad.

"And this man-thing stood up." Sorcerer rose slowly, to a crouch. "He grabbed a spear and threw it at my father." Sorcerer hurled an imaginary spear at Lefthand.

"I have that spearhead still, it's back in the tent. I use it for . . .

"Well, he threw it at my father. The spear grazed his leg, just tore the deerskin. Then the man-thing ran away in the storm and they forgot about him. They went to the fire and ate the meat. It was rat, only a little rat, and it made them hungrier. You know how." The three faces tilted up at Sorcerer and nodded understanding.

[136]

"And then they began to think about us, my mother and me and the other women, back here in the rock tent. What were they going to bring to us? They had eaten the rat. So, they went hunting for the man."

Sorcerer stalked around the fire, glancing left and right, brandishing his invisible spear.

"Father went along the cliff. He kept touching the cliff to guide himself. He stumbled on the man-thing." Sorcerer dropped to his knees and crawled past Jay, who drew back, startled by his expression of dull ferocity.

"It was creeping along like this, like some animal." Sorcerer leaped up. "Father jabbed like this" — he stabbed viciously downward — "and then" — relaxing — "he called the others. And they carried him back here."

Sorcerer faced the night. His eyes were wide and empty, as they must have been that day when he watched the extraordinary procession stumble in out of the storm. Gradually he came back to himself. His look brightened, humor lines creased his kindly face, and he sat down again.

Snowbird drew a long breath and asked, "What did you do?"

"What did we do? We ate him."

"You ate him?"

"Certainly." Sorcerer turned defiant eyes upon her. "Why not?"

Lefthand was much relieved to see the sorcerer's face return to its own good nature. He was wondering about this long-ago act of eating a little, hairy man — might this be the source of his magic? Perhaps the hairy one had possessed a magical power which Sorcerer had consumed.

Finally, wrestling inwardly with himself, Lefthand asked it.

"Is that why . . . why . . . why you are a sorcerer?"

"Is that why what? Oh yes, I see. It's not a thing everybody does, is it? Though I think more have done it than talk about it. No. The magic is another story. That was later, much later. It was summertime then, hot and bright. There were meat and fish on the racks and many families camped beside the river."

Lefthand forgot the cold and the dark around. He listened intently and his mind followed the words and the gestures away from winter, away from the rock tent, back to a distant summer.

He saw the summer river, wide and slow, reflecting a blue sky with puffy, friendly clouds. He saw the busy tent-town spread along the bank, bustling with smoke fires and talk and easy laughter. Children scampered about the camp. One of them was the little Sorcerer.

"One morning, a girl, one of my friends, was sick." Sorcerer told how she lay in the back of her mother's tent, her small face turned away from the light. She moaned and vomited while her friends squatted about, curious and puzzled. Then the mother came in, swatting left and right, and the boy who became the sorcerer ran away with the others into the bright, buzzing morning.

The children waded in shallow backwaters of the river. They caught minnows in their hands. They built stick tents on the bank and fashioned little clay men to live in them. Sheltered under the willows they slept through the noon glare. In the evening they straggled home to find the supper fires cold.

The mothers were gathered together in a tense, talking knot. In the middle of the knot was the tent where the sick girl lay. The children were hungry and puzzled. They remembered the sickness but the morning seemed long ago. Something had happened that they did not understand. Then came the fathers, masked for magic, with Sorcerer's father tapping his pigskin drum.

Half the night the men danced. The women talked, strangely quiet, and the children stood about watching, snacking on scraps of smoked fish and last night's dinner.

Firelight stretched the horn and antler shadows on the tent wall. Slowly the men forgot themselves, emptied their souls, until a child could not tell his father from his friend's father. It was good, strong magic, but it failed. As the moon rose the drum hesitated, then stopped, as the women folded the tent about the little dead girl and her father carried the bundle away.

"Then," Sorcerer went on, "it was a boy, my special friend. We had been spearing frogs together in the afternoon. The next morning he could not stand up."

As the summer days passed, one child after another could not stand up. The sick ones crawled into their mothers' tents, away from the light. There they trembled and vomited and often died. At night the children fell asleep to the drum music, their cheeks still warmed by their mothers' caressing fingers. Anxious mothers hovered and fluttered, astonishingly gentle.

One night Sorcerer's father put on a final, heartstopping show. He had a very special mask, a boar's head equipped with antlers. With this on his head he leaped and bounded about a sick child whose mother had brought him out to the fire. He yelled, he growled and snarled, he neighed and shrieked, and the men followed behind him, adding their noise to his. Surely now the Evil would hesitate. Surely it would draw back in fear and leave them alone.

In the morning the exhausted men held council beside the dead child. The Evil was not frightened. It was too strong for them. Sorceror's father advised that they should scatter. Then the Evil would have to choose one victim to follow. The rest would escape.

The men staggered to their tents and gave directions. The women folded the tents, bundled their goods on their backs, and they set out, each family alone.

With his parents Sorcerer passed the stagnant pools where he and his friends had played. Already the little stick tents were falling down, the clay men were damp, shapeless lumps scattered among gnawed bones and broken little spears.

"After that," Sorcerer concluded, "when we were alone, the Evil came hunting me."

"*You* were sick like the others?" Snowbird had not heard this story.

The old man nodded.

"But you didn't die!"

"No, my father chased the Evil away. He put on his boar mask and he danced by himself and the Evil let go and went away."

The audience sighed.

"But it left a mark where it bit me." Sorcerer suddenly raised his arms above his head. The cloak fell back, and the two arms stretched up bare in the firelight; one round, one like a gnarled branch. He pushed off one boot with the heel of the other, and thrust the withered, shrunken foot toward the fire.

Sorcerer looked around at them all to be sure they understood. Then he lowered his arms and pulled the boot back on. Summer faded from the rock tent. They were huddled once more about a tiny fire while snow piled up in bitter darkness a step away.

"So then," Lefthand pursued, wanting certainty, "you saw the power of magic, and you wanted to do it?"

"That, yes, but there was more than that. What kind of a hunter would I have made? Think of me chasing after reindeer on these legs or spearing bison with these arms." And the haggard old face broke into laughter. The sparse yellow teeth gleamed, the eyes creased to slits. The young people glanced at each other and laughed uncertainly.

"Put the meat in the fire," Sorcerer directed Snowbird. "We want more than stories of the past to warm us tonight!"

Snowbird reached behind her, grasped two frozen

carcasses, and slipped them into the embers. She cast a long look at her father, who sat silent, remembering.

Lefthand sat sniffing the roasting meat, enjoying the warmth close to his feet. He was thinking of the stories, turning them over in all the mental light he had. "We ate him," said Sorcerer's voice in his mind, "*why not?*"

Lefthand shivered as the old man had shivered and the tale turned slowly in the light of his understanding. Like a spearhead examined first in firelight, then in daylight, this story gave off a strange, dead glint. There was some reason *why not*. Lefthand felt there was and he suspected the sorcerer felt it, too. Why had he trembled, why had his eyes dilated at the memory?

A reason *why not* slept in the heart of humanity. It was there, but it slept so deeply that none of the four sheltered in the rock tent could awaken it.

SIX

THE MOUNTAIN

1

"COME IN," said the old man, "come on down!"
And he tittered. Sorcerer crouched in a hole in the
cliff, utter blackness behind him. His wrinkled face
peered up at Lefthand.

Bright winter sunshine bounced off the gray-white
rock and a fresh cold breeze slapped Lefthand's face.
He heard it hissing through the flames of the two pine
torches Snowbird held behind him on the rock path.
He heard her slight panting and felt her shoulder
brush his.

"Go," she whispered.

To find the magic, he must crawl into that dark hole away from the sun. Another moment of hesitation and the sorcerer would give him up — the chance would be lost. It was like throwing a spear. The time was Now. Lefthand took a deep breath, rested his weight on his hands, and swung his feet down into the dark.

Chuckling, Sorcerer held out a wizened hand. Snowbird leaned over the hole and handed down a torch. Desperately Lefthand looked at the sky, blue around her head, and at the brown stream of her hair, lifted by the wind and brightened like water by the sun. She smiled at him, handed down his torch, and whispered, "Go!"

The torch in his hand spat and dribbled. He clutched it as a starving man clutches meat, and turned into the darkness. Already the sorcerer was scrambling deep into the cliff. Lefthand saw him as a ragged shape against a spurting fountain of red light. Hastily Lefthand brought his own torch down to his knees to light the clay floor, and started after Sorcerer.

The cave instantly narrowed to a man's width. Lefthand bowed his head and bent his knees, squeezed between boulders, and climbed over rockfalls. He kept his eyes on the scurrying shape, the red light that waxed and waned ahead. Breathlessly he hurried after it and Fear hurried after him.

Once he glanced behind, and saw nothing but thick Dark. When he turned again the light ahead had vanished.

For an instant he saw its reflection on the damp clay wall facing him, then darkness. Only his own torch fought the Dark. As he hesitated, it flared and hot resin ran down his hand.

He glanced at the torch. It was half spent. Now Fear caught up with him, grabbed his throat. He could do one thing — turn back and run along the passage he had traveled. The torch might last as far as the hole, back to the wind and the sun.

He started to turn around.

Through the deep, chill stillness echoed a sudden sound, the old man's chuckle. Somewhere close by, the shriveled old creature was hunched up, shaking with mirth.

Lefthand's mind formed a picture. On the cave floor sat the sorcerer, cross-legged, like a hunter in a blind. He laughed to himself, gurgling between his few teeth. He was waiting for Lefthand to fall into a trap he had set. Perhaps in some deeper cavern his cooking fire already burned high and hot. "I can still scuttle around some, Provider! . . . I could surprise you with some of the things I eat! Hare, piglet, rat, or . . . anything that comes along."

Fury throttled Fear. Lefthand had no weapon but the dying torch. No matter, he could finish off the chuckling cannibal with his hands, then feel his way back to the light.

He dropped to his knees and one hand. He crawled silently forward. To one side he found the low hole through which his enemy had vanished. It was narrow. Lefthand thrust through the torch, then his head. Black water shone below. Would this be the trap? If he let himself down into that water, would he sink to the bottom of the mountain?

He waved the torch, trying to see into the water. Its reflection flared among ripples. Two torches burned in the water!

"Come on," said Sorcerer, "it's no deeper than your ankles." And he tittered again.

The sorcerer had crossed the water. There must be a way. Lefthand glanced again at the torch. It would last until he had killed the enemy and found his way back into the passage — if he acted quickly.

As he squirmed through the hole he saw Sorcerer.

Indeed, he was sitting cross-legged on the floor, grinning through his brown teeth.

"Come on," he urged, "the torches won't last forever."

In a spasm of anger Lefthand slithered through the hole, one hand holding the torch above his head. It *was* no deeper than his ankles. His feet splashed, hit bottom, and he stretched for the clay bank.

The old man bounced up. "Quick," he admonished, and scampered away down another passage.

Lefthand slipped and fell in the water. Both hands plunged. Darkness fell like a vast skin blanket as Lefthand dropped the dead torch in the water and leaped blindly for the bank. He scrambled up in time to see the bent figure, silhouetted by the torch, turn a corner.

Rushing, stumbling, banging into rock walls, Lefthand followed. The hoarse noise echoing around him was his breath. He could see nothing but the faint, last reflection of the torch. It seemed to stand still for him.

Gasping, he ran to seize the pale light on the rock. Suddenly strong light struck him forcibly from the side. He turned to look through a jagged hole in the wall, into a golden glow.

Blinking, he looked again. Before him the sorcerer stood erect, arms outstretched. On each palm he balanced a little sun, and by their quiet light he was illumined.

Over Sorcerer's shoulder a bison bull shook his mighty head and bellowed. Lefthand felt his roar but the sound was within himself, a rushing of exhaustion, anger, and fear down through his body to be lost in astonishment. The bull stretched sweeping horns across the rock wall toward a reindeer buck, who staggered and limped under a weight of well-aimed spears. Across his rump ran a pig, thrusting defiant little tusks. His black hind feet pointed to a pony who paused, head up and suspicious, hoofs lifting for flight.

All around the small circular cave animals plunged, trotted, and galloped. The earth should have shaken, the rock walls should have echoed their thundering strides. But it was only Lefthand who shook, only his thudding heart that echoed. The animals lived their startling, vibrant life on another plane; the actual cavern was still, so profoundly silent that even the whisper of the little suns roared in Lefthand's ears.

"Come in," said the sorcerer, and he held out one of the suns to Lefthand. It was a small, stone bowl, like those in his tent. In a pool of fat floated a twisted wick, and from this flickered the soft, sunny flame that warmed the cavern.

"Come on in," the old man repeated, his voice sober and solemn with no hint of titter or giggle. "You can do this, Lefthand. Provider told me."

Yes, Lefthand knew that he could do this. This was the one thing he could do; this was his magic. From his childhood he had worked this magic, sketching in sand or snow the prey his father followed. If his spear-hand was unsteady, his eye was faultless. He knew the forms of animals, he loved every line of them. In the dark cavern of his own mind he now found eager images forming; a pony mare cropped the last brown grass. He saw her mild eyes clearly, the fuzzy curve of her side, her shining hoofs. That image, welling from his mind, could flow through his hand onto stone, through stone, and back into reality.

The paintings were a dream of the sleeping earth; men would wake the earth, would make them real.

He looked at the blank spaces remaining on the stone walls and his hands ached to fill them. He looked at the sorcerer patiently holding out to him a gift of light. Did he know that Lefthand had followed him to kill him?

Lefthand laughed at himself a little grimly. He

bowed through the jagged entrance and took the gentle light in his hands.

2

The winter spent itself. Lefthand waked and came more alive each day, while in the depth of the cave, a creature slept. He dreamed of a spring hillside bright with brave flowers, rich with the scent of ant and grub and the hint of honey. In his dream he waggled his head, looked this way and that, and wondered which of many promising paths to take. Still he slept, pushing his huge head deeper into his warm flank, his claws scrabbling at the clay bed. He lay comfortably curled in utter darkness against a rough rock wall, his brown fur crushed against stone. No light ever reached this resting place, but the sleeper knew of passing time. His heart beat its passing and his fat shrank. Now he was beginning to feel empty, dissatisfied, and was almost conscious. Dim ghosts flitted in his brain whispering of hunger. He dreamed often and as he dreamed he moved, snuggled to himself, scratched his bed.

Not far away, Sorcerer laughed in delight. "I knew it," he cried. "I knew it when I saw you at the magic circle! I looked out and saw you sitting there, crumpled up like a leaf, and I saw it in your face. I said to myself, 'There is one who eats with his eyes!' "

He held a slab of stone to the lamp, gleefully examining the sketch scratched on its flat surface. It showed a reindeer fawn poised in profile. Head high, ears forward, he tasted the air.

"Eats with his eyes," Sorcerer had said. Lefthand stood beside his teacher, trying to maintain dignity and not hug himself or laugh! The fawn was good. It was really there in all its innocent strength. If he had killed and eaten it Lefthand would not have possessed it as he did now, and he understood quite well what the sorcerer meant. But he wanted to hear it said again. He wanted to be sure that there was one other human being in the world who felt like this.

"You and I," Sorcerer explained slowly, feeling for words, "we look at an animal and we take it inside our eyes, like meat. Only the animal is still there, outside us. He is himself, we are ourselves, you see, but we have him in us. So I say, we eat with our eyes. Every-

one does this, I think, but the others don't know they
do it. You and I, we know this secret."

Now Lefthand did hug himself. Impulsive in his
joy, he said, "I will tell you a secret, Sorcerer. I have a
friend who is a reindeer!" He pointed to the sketch.
"He looks like that."

Sorcerer nodded, not at all surprised. "Yes, that's
what I mean."

Encouraged, Lefthand went on to tell him about
the fever dream; the moonlit running, the search for
the doe, the lonesomeness. And Sorcerer kept
nodding.

"Yes, Lefthand, that is what I tell you. You do not
live in your stomach like my grandson Onedeer. He is
a fine young man, Onedeer, and he will kill more
animals than you will paint. His children will eat. But
he will never look at a fawn and see what you have
seen. For Onedeer, a fawn will never be anything
more than meat and hide and bone. But you, Lefthand, will live in your eyes and your heart. And
sometimes you will stretch out your heart like a hand
and reach beyond yourself." Sorcerer gave back the
sketch. "Now, go paint this on the wall. Paint it big,
strong. Then I will show you how to chisel it."

Lefthand took his stone lamp and his sketch. He

felt that he floated on joy, rather than walked, to the other side of the rock chamber. Here he had a space picked out and waiting — a narrow space, squeezed between two strange beasts. He set the lamp down on the floor and crouched beside it, drawing with his finger where he would make the actual soot lines.

These would be his first lines on the eternal wall of the earth's womb. Now, after all the sketches, he was ready. His practice slates were tossed here and there about the cavern floor. Mares were scratched on them, foals and pigs and bison. Through all the winter days Lefthand had been sketching, transferring to the stones all the brightness of his life in the shining, sunlit world above — or so he thought until he looked at the drawings a second time. Then he saw them as cold, fumbling lines, about as effective as the first babblings of a baby. And he cast them aside impatiently, not showing them to Sorcerer.

But Sorcerer would come limping along behind and pick them up and cluck over them.

"Why do you make only two legs?" he asked once, pointing scornfully, "I think most ponies have *four* legs."

"I know, I know," whined Lefthand, "but how can I draw the legs on the other side? You don't see through him."

"Look." And Sorcerer drew the legs for him, one bent behind another. Lefthand sucked his lips and nodded, while stars burst in his expanding mind.

Another time Sorcerer remarked, "You know, you can turn his head back over his shoulders . . . like this. You don't always see animals standing looking right ahead, like clay images."

"Mmm," said Lefthand, and got another slate.

This fawn was the first living, graceful animal he had made. And now it was time to take soot and ocher, and with his own trembling hand mark the deep of the world. A narrow jut of stone made a beautiful hind leg for the fawn — Lefthand had sketched it with this in mind —but it would cut through the head of one of the strange beasts.

"Sorcerer," Lefthand called, and his voice echoed loudly in the enclosed chamber, "what are these animals?"

Sorcerer was squatting near the entrance hole, chiseling the tail of a huge bull bison, and he did not stop work to look around. "I don't know," he said. "I have never seen any creature like them. There are more of those in the cavern across the passage."

"The holy one, where we don't go?"

"Yes."

"Is that why it is holy?"

"No, it is holy because men's bones lie there."

Lefthand studied the beasts. They marched across the wall, one behind the other, with majestic tread. Their bodies were wonderfully thick, heavier than those of pigs, and each had a second tail swinging from his head, and long, sweeping tusks.

"Someone has painted over these," he called. Indistinct ponies ran up and down through the huge bodies. "Can my fawn touch them?"

"Their magic is dead," came the brief reply. Lefthand dipped his finger in the hot soot of his lamp and began to draw.

The dreamer withdrew his head from his flank. He snuffled and waggled his ears. Sounds were attacking those ears, sinking into his dreams. An occasional dull roar became, in his dreams, his own voice, or that of a stream. But the harsh clinking sound that now accompanied the roar reminded him of nothing and called up no dream image. Then his stomach rumbled insistently and he opened one small eye.

"Sorcerer," Lefthand called. "This fawn is going to be strong magic!"

"I know that."

"I want to show it to Snowbird."

"*What?*"

Sorcerer rose, turned, and hobbled over to Left-hand. "You want to show it to *whom?*"

Puzzled, Lefthand looked up from the fawn's hind leg and saw the old man glaring down at him, being the Bear. But he knew the sorcerer too well now to be awed.

"I want to show it to your daughter, Snowbird."

Sorcerer slowly, dramatically, shook his head. "Oh no, Lefthand. You don't want to do that." He rested his hands on his knees and brought his face down to Lefthand's. More softly he explained, "Snowbird is a woman."

"Yes, I know."

"Soon she will have magic of her own, plenty of magic. You don't want to give her yours, too. You would have nothing left."

Uncomprehending, Lefthand stared up into the sharp old eyes. He thought of all women as being powerless, quite without magic. Bright had always seemed to him very little more important than he was himself — and that little, only because she was grown up. Now that he had found a source of power for himself, he wanted to share it with Snowbird as she had shared her fire and food with him. But the old man looked down at him with a brainful of memories, a heartful of power, and said: "No. No woman comes into this cave. Have you forgotten the little drum?"

The little drum. Oh yes, Lefthand remembered the secret, tender rhythm that he had tapped one night so that Snowbird could join the circle of women dancing to celebrate a mystery.

"You will never touch that drum again," said Sorcerer, straightening up. "You will never hear that beat again because you will soon be a man. Let Snowbird be a woman." And he turned away, chuckling at the amazement on Lefthand's face. Did Sorcerer know *everything?*

Sorcerer went back to his bison and Lefthand slowly drew the back of his fawn; the long, up-stretched neck, the stiffened ears. He stopped, got up, and stepped back to look. The line was perfect, living and alert. Lefthand gulped to quiet his excited stomach and stooped again to draw the fawn's chest and throat. He paused because his hand was shaking. He crouched down to look closely at his vision tangible on stone. As he did so, he heard a noise.

It came softly through the chisel noise. It was a noise such as Sorcerer sometimes made when he scratched a finished painting with an amazingly crude stone spearhead to soften and blend the colors. But

Sorcerer was not scratching now, he was chiseling with both hands, ding-ding-ding.

Lefthand heard a distinct scratching noise.

"Sorcerer!" he called, and the walls repeated it. "What made that sound?"

"Sound?" asked Sorcerer above the clink of the chisel. "You'll be making this sound yourself when you finish that painting!" Clank, clank, clank, said the chisel, and again a scratch whispered between blows.

"I heard a scratch," said Lefthand, and his voice shook.

"A scratch?" Sorcerer paused and looked around. As the echo of the chisel died, the scratching became clearly audible.

Sorcerer turned pale. In the flickering lamplight Lefthand saw his face fade to the whiteness of the very rock behind him. He whispered "a spirit!" and the whisper echoed "spirit!"

Lefthand was suddenly conscious of the immense, silent mountain all about them. It was honeycombed with caverns, passages, underground streams, of which he knew only this room and the two passages that led to it. The chambers were endless. Even Sorcerer did not know them all.

Some of the near rooms, like the one across the passage, were holy. Men had died there and bones lay stretched on the rock floors. In imagination Lefthand now saw those bones sitting up, the dry fingers brushing the stones. With shaking hands he snatched up his lamp. The bones were out in the dark; the vast, waiting dark. In the face of a spirit, the light in his hands was better than a spear.

Sorcerer picked up his own lamp. He turned to face the low, jagged entrance through which the bones would have to come.

In the silence that followed the scratching, the only sound was of their teeth chattering uncontrollably.

The sleeper was now fully awake. He stood up swaying, weak and bewildered. He was very, very hungry.

He strained his eyes into the dark. They were not good eyes in any light. He relied more upon his nose and his nose told him food was near.

He swung his sagging bulk toward the smell and stumbled forward, feeling his way. He staggered against the rock wall, rubbed his side against it, then rose on his hind legs and scratched the rock. It felt good to sharpen his claws; it sent pleasant tingles through his paws and forelegs. His muscles awoke.

As he scratched, luxuriously stretching to his full

height and drawing his sleep-dulled claws along the rock, the clinking noise stopped.

Now the smell of living flesh became very strong and acrid. It annoyed his nose — it angered him, and roused in him an itch to destroy. He dropped to his four legs and moved purposefully toward the smell of fear.

Light surprised him. He had not expected to see the sun! But this was not the sun. It was a small light flickering through a hole. He would have passed it by, blinking and looking away, but the smell of flesh and of fear came out of this hole.

Squinting, he pushed his head into the light.

Lefthand dropped his lamp. He stood stupefied by terror. The huge, hairy head thrust in through the entrance, the slits of eyes and gleaming teeth, was more dreadful to him than any skeleton. He could have attempted to fight off the dead. But this was the face that he still saw in the depths of frequent night-mares. If he had been alone, the bear could have pushed in and devoured him.

Sorcerer heard the crash of the stone lamp hitting the floor and knew what it meant without looking. The light was brighter now, as the spilled fat flared, and the bear closed his eyes against it and opened his long, black jaws. From his throat came a whining growl.

In that moment Sorcerer felt relief. So it was a bear coming out of his winter sleep who scratched in the darkness. It was not a ghost, the ghost of his father, become alien and hostile in the strange realm of death; not a small, hairy ghost with tremendous, humped shoulders; and not his woman come to find him, impatient with her long, long wait. It was only a bear, an animal, who could be fought. Sorcerer's teeth stopped chattering.

Lefthand watched, unable to move, as Sorcerer walked straight up to the bear, holding his lamp towards its face.

"Go out," said Sorcerer gently to the bear. "Go on up to the sun. Go out of this cave. There is nothing for you here." He waved the lamp close to the bear's nose.

The bear's head withdrew and a huge paw swung through the hole and whacked at the lamp. Sorcerer let the paw hit the lamp but held onto it firmly. Burning fat spattered all around. Just outside the hole the black jaws opened and howled. The howl echoed through the caverns, bouncing from depth to depth.

"Go up to the sun," Sorcerer kept insisting, waving

the lamp in the hole to keep out the jaws. "Go up on the mountain."

The bear pulled his burned paw back through the opening and licked it. His huge tongue, lapping at the hurt, uttered an astonishing sound — a whimper, a baby's complaint. Lefthand found he could move. He stooped and picked up the spilled lamp.

The bear might try again. Lefthand knew he was needed. Sorcerer's lamp had been spilled now and less than half the fat remained in the bowl. Lefthand's lamp was almost empty but a tiny flicker of flame wavered at the bottom. He must add this light to Sorcerer's.

Holding the lamp out before him in both hands, Lefthand took a step away from the wall. The face in the hole bared its teeth and snarled at him. Lefthand stopped, trembling. Then he realized that the bear could not see him through the light thrust before its eyes. He made himself move forward again.

Sorcerer was talking. Lefthand slowly became conscious of his words. In the same gentle, soothing tone he was saying, "Go on up, go up on the mountain, bring me that light, there is food out there, none here, hurry up, up on the mountain you will find food, my light is dying."

The cadence of his words was like a soft drumbeat.

Lefthand stepped to its beat and came up by Sorcerer's shoulder before he realized where he was. There was the gigantic, fearful head right in front of him, the paw beginning to reach out again as Sorcerer's light sank feebly.

Lefthand took one look in the bear's face and did not look again. Quickly he tipped the remainder of his burning grease into Sorcerer's bowl. The combined flames reared up, piercing the dark with writhing red pain. The bear made his decision.

Whatever the morsel in that hole, it bit too hard. He moaned querulously to himself and turned away. The face vanished from the hole, leaving a blank darkness. Lefthand heard the click of the bear's claws on the stone passage, moving away.

They stood together, panting. "Will he go out?" asked Lefthand.

"Yes. I told him to."

"Will he wait for us in the passage?"

"No, no. He's too hungry to wait for anything. He just woke up."

Mentally, Lefthand followed the bear's progress up the passage . . . through the water . . . through the hole to the upper passage . . . along the winding way toward the light.

"Sorcerer!" His cry echoed again through the painted room. "He will meet Snowbird out there!"

Sorcerer stared at Lefthand. His face, which had regained color paled again to a sickly gray. "The mountain is wide," he muttered. "She may be far away."

"She and Jay will be at the entrance. They are there every evening!"

Sorcerer's eyes, wild and shallow, darted around the room. They had brought no weapons with them into the holy place. "Take stones," he mumbled, his tongue thick and slow. "Stones are all we have."

Lefthand dropped his unwieldy bowl at Sorcerer's feet. He rushed around the room, collecting his scribble stones from the floor. Scratched with rough, amateurish attempts, they had only a little magic; but they were his hope. An armful of these stones would do the bear little or no harm, but the magic might deter him. It was their only chance.

Lefthand charged first out of the hole, the stones clasped in his arms and one in his fist. Sorcerer followed, holding the weak lamp.

Lefthand ran along the passage, chasing his own furious shadow cast by the sputtering light behind him. He could see only a few steps ahead and suddenly remembered his former fear: will he wait for us in the passage? He no longer cared. If the bear were waiting, Snowbird might hear the uproar and retreat from the entrance.

But the bear was not in the passage nor sitting in the water as Lefthand had fleetingly imagined. Fresh claw marks in the clay of the opposing wall showed where he had crawled through the hole to the upper way, moments before.

As though he had all his life been sound and healthy, Lefthand plunged through the water, caught hold of the threshold and dragged himself up in the space of a breath. He waited in darkness while Sorcerer splashed to him through the stream. The light in the old man's hand came through the hole. "You take it," he heard Sorcerer say. "You'll get there faster."

Lefthand did not pause to answer. He seized the faint light and rushed along the stone corridor, dodging around boulders, squeezing between pinched walls. At one point he saw claw marks on the clay where he set his own hand; at a narrowing of the passage long hairs brushed from the rock onto his arm.

He started up the sharp, uphill pitch to the track. Then Lefthand saw the bear.

He was standing under the ragged hole that led out

of the mountain. Like a fat man he stood upright, both hands on the edge just above his head. Lefthand saw his rounded head with the little round ears and the outline of the tilted jaw silhouetted against daylight.

Lefthand stopped dead. The bear was not doing any harm. He need not be attacked. At the prospect of not having to attack, Lefthand felt all his fear return, flooding his system like a sudden sickness. That would not do; the bear would surely smell it, and turn. Lefthand relaxed, breathing softly, and tried to watch the bear.

The bear whined to himself and moaned and snarled at the effort required to lift himself up to the light. Snowbird must have heard his noise and been well away by now. Lefthand pictured her cowering behind a boulder hugging Jay, probably with a hand clapped to his mouth.

Grabbing firm hold of the rock ledge the bear scrabbled with his hind feet. His claws dug into the clay, his bottom wiggled hugely as with a gigantic heave he hoisted himself up through the hole.

Light vanished, blocked by the huge shape who sat on the edge looking around, blinking and snuffing the early spring wind.

It was too soon for honey. There was still thin snow

coating the mountain, but grass was growing down in the valley. There would be ants moving about among the young roots.

The bear grunted and got up on four shaky legs. Weakly he started downhill toward the hope of ants and grubs. His empty stomach swung beneath him as he walked and his brown coat, shining in the evening light, wrinkled over his shoulders. It was too big for him by a whole season.

As in his dream, he swung his head and tested the cold spring air and hints of food came strongly now from the valley. He lumbered faster down the slope, among tiny bright flowers pushing up through the snow. Shuffling and shambling, his shape dwindled to a reddish spot moving slowly across the green valley floor.

Snowbird raised her hand from Jay's mouth and he burst into words. "He didn't get them! Did you see his stomach? Empty!"

Snowbird dodged from behind the boulder and ran to the hole in the cliff. She wondered as she ran if she dared go in, just a little way into the blackness, or if she dared call. She leaned over the hole and Lefthand's welcome face grinned up at her.

His face changed as she looked; the triumphant grin faded, softened, shifted, and became a smile.

Snowbird had never seen Lefthand smile before. As a little boy he had been serious, grave, and shy, and since the bear tore him he had been grim. She marveled at the warmth of his smile, the light of it.

"Lefthand," she said uncertainly, "is that you?"

"No," said Sorcerer, his voice rising out of the dark behind Lefthand. "Not exactly. He is not exactly the same Lefthand. He has gone far beyond himself."

3

The cliff wall sparkled in strong, spring sunshine. Directly beneath a jutting overhang of rock gleamed a circle of warm mud. A plump young doe pawed and circled there. She had scraped up seedling grass and spring-soft earth, and her restless hoofs had churned the warm spot to mud. Still she circled, keeping her nose to the center of the new mud bed. She panted, staring around with pain-startled eyes. Buckling her knees, at last she knelt and lay down. She stretched, opened her mouth, and groaned.

She had chosen a quiet place, sheltered from the

slow-moving herd. In front she was screened by low bushes, at her back rose the sheer cliff wall. In her dim mind, overwhelmed by urgent surprise, the place was safe.

Jay leaned round-eyed over the edge of the cliff path. Snowbird's firm hand on his shoulder shushed him. Painter slid down cross-legged beside her, and the three of them leaned across the overhang together, looking down in utter silence.

Close beneath them the young doe stretched and panted behind her screen of bushes. They saw the bright brown of her summer coat, the flash of her flickering tail. They saw the wild eyes staring, her sides bulging like a tightly packed skin bag.

Beyond the greening bushes moved a hundred brown backs. Slowly the herd of north-returning reindeer browsed up the valley. Every one of the females showed a tight, swollen belly. They would all give birth soon. Then when the newborn fawns could run, they would again move northward.

Close by, several heavy does folded their legs and lay down to chew their cud. Munching peacefully, they looked out over the soft spring valley to the river, flowing blue under a blue sky. Like a strip of sky fallen to earth, it wandered down the valley, pausing here, curving there among the willows.

Far across the valley two brown specks stood against the cliffs. One, expanding and heaving, was a migrating herd, perhaps of bison. The other speck was the camp.

Painter sat up straight and thrust back his shoulders. Images of the future crowded into his mind. He saw the valley as it would be when again the sun faded and the year died. He saw the cluster of tents growing, reaching tattered tentacles toward the river. Down from the far forests came the people, downriver from the north came the reindeer.

The big drum boomed. Painter saw himself dancing in a horned mask. He saw himself with other young men striding away into the forest. They were vague shadows except for one who might be Onedeer. He saw Snowbird pulling the baggage sled.

Another figure insisted on prancing into the picture. It would not be left out. It was a small figure that ranged, puppylike, around Snowbird. Sometimes it helped to pull the sled, more often it stole a ride.

Another figure came limping after the departing group. It stumbled and waved long thin arms. White hair drifted about its head, like the ruff of an ancient, hardy reindeer.

"Sorcerer is old . . . and he was never strong."

Painter scowled to himself as the shadowy young

men of his daydream strode on and away, out of the scene. He saw himself hesitate, pause, then turn back. He could walk all day now; he could hurl a spear and sometimes hit the mark. Sorcerer's wisdom had given him back the strength he once had, and more. Sorcerer had also taught him to reach beyond himself.

In the daydream, the Painter came back to the floundering, white-haired figure. There were words, gestures, a decision. The party turned back toward the valley, toward the river, the traps, and the dark magic caverns.

Painter glanced at Snowbird beside him. She was looking intently down. His gaze followed hers.

The doe was straining. She had given up feeling or wondering and now she was doing what she had come there to do. She raised her nose to the sky, arched her back, and groaned with effort. Then she panted quietly until another wave of pain seized her. Again she raised her nose and her back, and she groaned.

Stretched out on his stomach on the cliff, Jay dislodged a small stone that rattled down beside the doe. She paid no attention; she had no ears or eyes now for anything outside herself. The other does resting beside the cliff looked up and waved hairy ears. Snowbird's hand on Jay's shoulder squeezed a warning.

Now, under the doe's raised tail, appeared a slight,

gray bulge. Her groans loudened to roars of spent energy that echoed from the cliff. Again she strained, and the gray bulge pushed slowly out, weaving as it came.

A moment of rest followed. The emerging ooze lay motionless along the ground and Painter could see through the slime the outline of a small head. Its nose rested on little, soft hoofs. Its eyes bugged blindly.

The doe scrambled to her feet, dangling the fawn. One last effort, and it was born. It flopped to the ground and lay inert, still encased in slime. It was long and thin, built for speed. Not yet breathing, the flat body seemed dead.

The doe turned around and nosed the small thing. With her tongue she licked the slime away from its head. As Bright would lift the skin from a carcass, so the doe's tongue lifted the birth-skin from the blunt little nose. As she was licking its eyes the fawn sneezed. Its head waved, its mouth opened, and it uttered a shrill, high bleat.

The doe grunted to it reassuringly. As she licked, she kept muttering. "Keep away," she said to the world, and to the fawn, she said, "I am here."

The reindeer near the bushes looked toward the sounds, the high bleatings and gentle mutterings. They were all pregnant does, and these sounds waked strong instincts in them. This fawn was the first born of the herd. Before nightfall, there would be several more.

The cliff path was now hot under the noon sun. Jay and Snowbird rested motionless, the two profiles leaning together, one soft with childish curves, the other sharp and brooding. Painter was fingering a small slate. He had scratched on the rock at his knee a hasty outline of the straining doe. Now he chose a smaller stone, and scratched the human profiles.

It came hard. The curve of cheek, the jut of nose, were clear to his eye. But somewhere between eye and hand they came undone. He tried again. "One spear at a time," he thought. "Snowbird first."

The forehead, nose and chin came out right. Hard on the gray stone appeared a thin, pale line, a chalky image of Snowbird's brown warmth. Weak magic.

Below, the fawn was struggling to stand. Its foreparts were dry now, almost fluffy. Its eyes saw, its ears pricked. Even while the doe licked its back legs it was flopping around on the front ones. As if it knew that danger threatened it now, and always would, the infant deer was determined to find its feet.

"Wait," the doe's mutterings meant, "wait till I get this last bit."

The fawn stood up. It wavered, and when the doe licked its shoulder, it collapsed.

Magic had brought dream to reality. Sleeping through the winter, the earth had dreamed of reindeer.

In its depths silent herds thundered. Wakened by spring, earth produced reindeer: round, hairy does that munched, browsed, and gave birth.

Now the little one was searching along its mother's side, sucking at hairs. The doe stood still and content in the sunshine. Gently she licked her fawn till its hair stood up in springy curls. Its tail jerked joyfully. It had found milk.

Painter looked again at the smooth stone at his knee. He looked at the cold, chalky line that suggested Snowbird. He would need no magic with Snowbird. But suppose someone else found this drawing? With fingers and slate Painter pried the magic stone loose from the cliff path. Snowbird watched curiously as he stood up and swung, throwing it far away to where it would never be found.

The stone fell in a heap of loose stones under the cliff. There in the flow of endless time, it would become a deep, infinitesimal part of the mountain.